THIN WOOD WALLS

THIN
WOOD
WALLS

David
Patneaude

Houghton Mifflin Company Boston 2004

To Judy with the generous heart;
to Jaime, Jeff, and Matt, who have given me so much;
and to the turbulent year 1944, when life was darker but simpler,
and Dave, Mike, and Billy first came unstuck in time.

Copyright © 2004 by David Patneaude

www.houghtonmifflinbooks.com

The text of this book is set in 11-point Californian.

Library of Congress Cataloging-in-Publication Data
Patneaude, David.
Thin wood walls / by David Patneaude.
p. cm.
Summary: When the Japanese bomb Pearl Harbor, Joe Hanada and his family
face growing prejudice, eventually being torn away from their home and sent
to a relocation camp in California, even as his older brother joins the United
States Army to fight in the war.
ISBN 0-618-34290-7
1. Japanese Americans—Evacuation and relocation, 1942–1945—Juvenile fiction.
[1. Japanese Americans—Evacuation and relocation, 1942–1945—Fiction.
2. World War, 1939–1945—United States—Fiction.] I. Title.
PZ7.P2734Th 2004   [Fic]—dc22   2004001014

ISBN 13: 978-0-618-34290-7

Manufactured in the United States of America
MP 10 9 8 7 6 5 4 3 2 1

Acknowledgments

Thanks to those who made it possible for me to piece together the background of this story: the good folks at the White River and Wing Luke Museums and the Bellevue, Bothell, Kent, Kingsgate, Woodinville, and University of Washington libraries; the members of the Tule Lake Committee and their beautiful publication of photos and remembrances, *Second Kinenhi: Reflections on Tule Lake*; the White River Valley Chapter of the Japanese American Citizens League and its *Pictorial Album of the History of the Japanese of the White River Valley*; Stan Flewelling, who has documented so thoroughly the early history of Japanese Americans in the Pacific Northwest in his wonderful book *Shirakawa*; and the residents of Newell, California, who were kind enough to point out landmarks and the ghostly remains of what was once the Tule Lake War Relocation Center.

Special thanks to all those who gave me their time for interviews and who provided me with documents, photos, memories, and encouragement: Carl and George Iseri, who sat with me in the middle of a family gathering and told their stories; George Iwasaki, who served in the 442nd and lived to tell about it; Jane Ikeda, who took an interest in what I was doing and helped with research; Jana (Ikeda) Hammerquist and her husband, Greg, my neighbors and friends; Roy Ikeda, who shared what it was like to return from exile; Mae Yamada, who has been an untiring source of information on the experience of Japanese Americans of the White River Valley, not just for me but for the community as well; Carolyn Yamada, who let me borrow her husband and crash her party; and my friend, guide, and inspiration, Doug Yamada, without whom this book simply wouldn't have happened.

Special special thanks to Emilie Jacobson, who found a home for the story; to Andrea Davis Pinkney, who gave it a home; and to Emily Linsay, who worked hard and expertly to make it better.

PART ONE

December moonlight

On fallow fields; clouds blooming,

Lightning in their midst.

ONE

I didn't like the back seat of our old Ford, and I avoided it whenever I could. Sitting short and low, I could only see where we were, but I wanted to be the first to see where we were going. And riding in back made me carsick in a hurry, especially on winding roads like the one we were on now.

So I was happy to be up front with Dad and Mom, cheek against the cool glass, looking ahead. The window was rolled down an inch, allowing me to breathe in a small but steady stream of fresh December air.

"Where are we going?" I said for the second, or maybe the third, time.

"You will see," Dad said. Mom smiled.

From the back seat came my big brother Mike's voice, falsely squeaky, mocking me: "Where are we going?"

"Hush, Michael," Mom said.

Grandmother's voice rose behind me: "You have the patience of a puppy, Joseph."

"How soon will we be there?" I said.

Grandmother made a sound in her throat. Dad chuckled. He shook his head. "Soon, Joseph."

I settled back. I could be patient. I watched as we turned from one quiet road to another, heading into the green hills east of our valley. I wondered what time it was. First there had been church and a long sermon from Reverend Sakamoto. Now this. How much longer would I have to wear this suit and tie? How much time would I have for my writing once we finally got home?

The road wound into groves of evergreens and flattened out. We lost sight of farmland and houses. Dad slowed the car and leaned forward, peering down the right shoulder. I leaned also, eyes wide open, looking. For what?

Finally he braked and turned right, onto a two-rut dirt road, dark in the shadow of forest on either side, quiet like a graveyard. Were we lost?

"Where are we?" Mike said.

"The deepest jungle," Dad said, and I pictured fierce beasts — wolves and bears and mountain lions—lurking nearby, eyeing us, licking their slobbery lips.

A month earlier my teacher, Mrs. Lynden, had asked me to write our class's Thanksgiving play. I leaped at the chance, staying inside, staying up late, writing a story about the first Thanksgiving. I didn't write about wild beasts in the woods. But if I were rewriting the play, I would add a scene: brave Pilgrims struggling through a gloomy forest thick with ferocious animals.

We inched around a bend in the road, then another. It grew lighter. We came to a broad field of thick stumps, and growing among them, small trees.

Dad stopped the car and turned off the engine. Before he could open his door, I was out, ready to see it, whatever it was.

Mike jumped out next. Why didn't Grandmother ever needle *him* about impatience? The rest of the car emptied—Dad, then Mom, then Grandmother, stubbornly struggling to her feet on her own.

Dad wore a small smile. Mom, too. Grandmother and Mike shared a puzzled look. I tried to look patient. I tried not to dance from foot to foot.

"Put these on," Mom said. She took Mike's everyday shoes, then mine, from a bag. We sat on the Ford's running board and made a quick change.

"Come," Dad said, taking Grandmother's arm. We stepped away from the car, our breath clouding the chilly air.

Dad pulled a white handkerchief from his suit coat pocket. "This land belongs to the Spooners," he said.

I looked around at the greens and browns stretching off in every direction. I heard the calls of birds. I smelled the wet, wintry smells of land that God had made. I closed my eyes and imagined. I liked to write haiku, a kind of Japanese poetry often linked to nature, and I wanted to remember this place. It was the kind of setting where haiku could take root. "It would be good to own this property," I said.

Grandmother made a sour face. "*Tochi-ho,*" she spat.

Suddenly I was sorry I'd said anything. I didn't know much Japanese, but I knew that *tochi-ho* meant land law. Issei, immigrants from Japan—like my parents, like my grandmother—were forbidden by law to own land.

"Mr. Spooner made me a kind offer," Dad said, ignoring his

mother's words. "He said we should choose our Christmas tree from these young ones. No charge."

A Christmas tree. We had never cut our own. I imagined finding the perfect one. I felt a warmth fill my chest. My feet itched to move. "Where's the saw?" I asked Dad. I couldn't wait to cut our tree from the real woods and take it home. I couldn't wait to show it to my friend Ray O'Brien.

Dad smiled, patiently. "Today is not the cutting day, Joseph. Today is the choosing day." He held up the handkerchief. "You and Michael may select a tree now, and mark it with this for when we return."

Mike took the handkerchief. "Let's go find a prizewinner, Joe." He marched off; I rushed to catch up.

"I should help them choose," Grandmother said behind me. She sounded serious, but Dad laughed. I sped up, just in case, and Mike stayed in front of me, high-stepping. It would take us all day to find a tree if Grandmother helped us.

There were hundreds of trees, but some were too tall for our living room, others were too short, too skinny, too sparse, too lopsided. Finally I found one that looked good. I proudly pointed it out to Mike.

"Hemlock," he said. "It would lose half its needles the first day."

We crossed the road, still searching.

"Maybe Mr. Spooner knew there were no Christmas trees here," Mike said.

"There are plenty," I said. "We just haven't found the perfect one."

I hurried off on my own, wondering how much time Dad would give us. I came to a huge stump, nearly my height, more than ten feet across, and scrambled onto it.

Standing, brushing wet debris from my suit, I noticed a promising clump of trees on the other side of a little knoll. I jumped down and headed toward them.

And that's where I found it.

"Mike!" I yelled, circling the tree.

He was there in an instant. "It's a fir, at least," he said, shadowing me as I went around and around, examining it up and down. "The right height," he added. "Straight trunk, lots of branches, even growth, good color."

We stopped circling. I waited for him to find something wrong with my tree. I held my breath.

"It's a beauty, Joe," he said finally, and I breathed, deep. "It's gonna make a swell Christmas tree." He knotted Dad's handkerchief snugly around the end of a high branch and patted me on the head. The sweet smell of bruised fir needles filled my nose.

We waved to Mom, Dad, and Grandmother. We pointed at the tree and they clapped. Smiles lit their faces.

"Joe found a prize!" Mike yelled, and I looked at my tree, uneasy about leaving it.

"Can we take it home today?" I asked when we got back to the car. "Someone else could find it."

"Not today, Joseph," Dad said. "The tree will begin dying as soon as it loses its roots."

"We will come back," Mom said. "It will still be here."

"If it is not," Grandmother said, "there are others."

"Not like this one, Grandmother," Mike said. "Joe found the champ."

"Still..." Dad said, and began moving toward the car.

The discussion was over. I looked once more, hoping I could

see the tree, hoping I couldn't. From fifty yards away, the white handkerchief glowed against the green.

Ray was sitting on our front porch steps when we got home. He had his battered basketball under his arm, dreams of playing for the University of Oregon in his head. I saw them reflected in his eyes as I got out of the car.

"How was St. Paul's, Joe?" He unfolded his long frame and stood.

"We found a Christmas tree, Ray!" I blurted out.

"At church?"

"On Mr. Spooner's property. He's letting us cut one."

"It's a beauty," Mike said.

"Super," Ray said, eyeing the Ford's trunk.

"No one asked for my opinion," Grandmother said from inside the car.

"We don't have the tree yet," I said to Ray. "A tree starts dying as soon as it's cut. We're going back for it in two weeks. Maybe you can come."

"Of course he can," Mom said.

"Great," Ray said.

"Perhaps someone will ask for my opinion," Grandmother said, louder. She sat at the edge of the back seat, short legs dangling out.

Dad said something to her in Japanese, and her frown disappeared. "Grandmother will choose where to put the tree," he said. I decided that would be okay. Grandmother had an artist's eye.

"Shoot some baskets, Joe?" Ray said. "Mom invited you to lunch."

"Yeah!" I said, before I thought to ask.

"Joseph was very fidgety in church, Raymond," Mom said, and

my hopes cooled. For a moment I'd thought that this was going to be a perfect day. "You must promise to tire him out."

I felt myself smile. Dad, usually quick to ask Ray about his family, just nodded and went into the house.

"I promise, Mrs. Hanada," Ray said.

"Soon as I change," I said.

"You too, Mike," Ray said. Mike was trying to help Grandmother out of the car.

"You go shoot the baskets, Michael," she said, standing straight. "I am not a cripple."

"We can make Joe chase rebounds," Ray told him.

"Funny," I said.

"Good idea," Mom said.

"Not now, Ray," Mike said. Like Dad, he seemed preoccupied. He was sixteen, but considered himself an adult. He'd been taking part in the late-night discussions with my parents and grandmother and their friends and had gotten good at solemn faces, whispers, keeping me out of things.

I wasn't sixteen. I was eleven and according to Grandmother, cursed with impatience. But I wasn't impatient to grow up, to have to wear a long face. This was December. Kids my age were supposed to think only of what that meant: Christmas and presents, vacation from school. Snow, although snow seldom came to the White River Valley. If I was impatient, it was for those things.

But I was drawn to the whispers as a moth is drawn to a candle flame, seeking the light, suffering the heat. The more I learned, the hotter the world seemed, the darker. Two days earlier, Friday evening, I had paused outside the kitchen long enough to hear Mom, Dad, Mike, and Grandmother talking about a subject that these days seemed to hang in the air like ground fog, smelling of unseen things rotting.

"Germany?" Dad was saying. "Germany we know about."

"And it's all bad," Mike said.

"Still…" Dad said.

"Germany is the single-edged sword," Mom said. "We know where it will cut."

"It's cutting the world in half," Mike said.

"And it must be stopped," Dad said. "But a bigger concern for us is the unknown. When will the United States enter the war? And once that happens, what will Germany's ally in the Pacific—Japan—do?"

"Japan is the double-edged sword," Mom said. "War with Japan will hurt not just the United States, but us as a people. Once our country and Japan are enemies, what will *we* be? What will our neighbors think of us? What will the government do about us?"

"Government," Grandmother echoed. She had no love for government—ours or Japan's. Her husband, an innocent bystander, had been killed by government policemen during a political disturbance at a Tokyo park in 1905. Grandmother had been a widow ever since. Dad had been a half orphan.

"Will we be treated as Americans?" Dad said. "Or as Japanese?"

"We *are* Americans," Mike said. "Joe and I are citizens."

"Citizens," Grandmother said. "Yes." But she didn't sound convinced, or convincing. Issei were not only forbidden to own land, they also couldn't become citizens here. I slipped away, burning with worry. I had come too close to the flame.

By Sunday, though, war talk had been pushed to the corners

of my mind again. War was something I would rather not think about.

Twenty minutes after I got home from church and the Christmas tree adventure, Ray and I had run the half-mile to his house and were out on our deluxe basketball court.

Months before, Ray's dad had mounted a rim and backboard on the sturdy trunk of a cottonwood, and Ray and I did the rest. Ground clearing. Weed pulling. Rock mining. Driving the tractor back and forth to pack the dirt.

I wasn't tall and Ray was. He could shoot and dribble with both hands and grab rebounds. But I could shoot, too, and I was quicker. Most days I kept our games close.

I challenged him to a game of one on one. We flipped a penny for first outs. Ray won the toss, but I wouldn't let one little thing ruin a perfect day. He took the ball and backed me toward the hoop, dribbling side to side, his usual tactic.

"Come on, big man," I said. "Go straight at me, face to face."

"And let you steal it?" But suddenly he pivoted and drove, me on his hip. He started up for a shot, but ended up without the ball. I'd swiped it away.

"You got it down in dangerous territory," I said, dribbling back out. "Joe territory."

"Yeah?" he said. "Yeah? Yeah?" He charged at me, out of control, and I went around him for an easy lay-up.

"I'll give you that one," he said. "But you need nine more."

"At least your arithmetic's good," I said.

"Yeah. And my arithmetic says I'm eight inches taller than you." He started backing me down again, protecting the ball. There wasn't much I could do.

"And eight hours slower," I said.

He backed me all the way under the basket and banked in an easy shot. "Tied, speedy," he said.

We kept playing, sweating and laughing, trading baskets. With the game tied at nine each, Ray missed a shot. I beat him to the rebound and dribbled out with him on me close, long arms waving in my face. I faked a drive and went up for a shot. The ball left my hand, and his hand came down hard across my arm. The shot went in, then out, and Ray grabbed the rebound.

"I fouled you," he said, handing me the ball.

"After the shot," I said, adjusting my glasses on my nose. "It didn't matter."

"Your ball," he said. "Take it out."

"No," I said. "I missed the shot. You rebounded." I tried to hand the ball back to him, but he wouldn't take it. I let it drop to the ground.

Ray stared at the ball, then up at the bare limbs of the cottonwood, as if something were there. "Nine–nine" he said. "Let's call it a game." He took a deep breath, slow, through his nose. "I think I smell lunch."

Ray's nose was right. Good smells—roast beef and fresh-baked bread—lured us to the house.

We'd just gotten to the back door when his mom appeared, looking like she'd been slapped. She tugged at the neck of her sweater as if she didn't know what to do with her hands. Ray's dad stood behind her, wearing the same wounded expression. I heard radio sounds—a newsman's voice.

"You boys come and eat," Mrs. O'Brien said. "Then we're going to walk Joe home."

"There's been some bad news," Mr. O'Brien said.

I searched their faces for clues. Had something happened to my parents? Mike? Grandmother?

"What?" Ray's round freckled face took on the gray color of the sky.

Ray's parents looked at each other, frozen, their big bodies filling the doorway. Finally Mrs. O'Brien spoke up. "We thought we should wait for your folks to tell you, Joe. But I don't want you to worry over the wrong things." She leaned down, hands on my shoulders, and looked me gently in the eye. And kept looking, too long.

"What happened?" I said. "What's wrong?"

"Your family's fine," she said. She swallowed, and a tear squeezed from the corner of her eye and eased down her cheek. "But we just heard on the radio that the Japs…the Japanese… have bombed us, bombed our military bases in Hawaii."

"They sank our ships," Mr. O'Brien said. "Big ones. Lots of 'em. Killed hundreds, maybe thousands, of our sailors."

I couldn't believe it. "Maybe it's not true," I said. "Maybe it's make-believe, like that radio show about men from Mars." I strained to hear what the man on the radio was saying, but Mr. O'Brien walked into the house and switched it off.

"Yeah," Ray said. "Why would Japan bomb us? We're not in the war." His voice was shaking, tears were building up on his bottom eyelids.

His mom put her arm around his shoulders. "We don't know. But it's not make-believe. We checked other radio stations. Your dad called his friend at the *Seattle Times*."

I'd lost my appetite; I just wanted to be with my family. I wondered if they knew, if I should call them. But we went in and washed up and sat down—Ray, his mom and dad, his little brother, Henry, and me. Everyone took some food. Henry, who was safe in his five-year-old world, began eating.

But I couldn't stay. I pushed out my chair and stood. "I have to go," I said. "Sorry." I headed for the door, grabbing my coat on the way out, but the O'Briens were right behind me.

"It's okay, Joe," Mrs. O'Brien said, her voice fading. I was hurrying, but Ray caught up with me, and Henry managed to take the lead, half-running, half-skipping.

We were close to my house when I saw three familiar figures approaching. I took off running. I zoomed past Henry and waded into Mom's arms, then Dad's. Mike stood there, hands jammed in his pockets, anger on his face. The muscles in his thick neck bulged out like bamboo stalks. He put a hand on my shoulder as I looked around. Up and down our street, people—Japanese American and white—were out in front of their houses, clustered in small groups. Separate groups.

The O'Briens caught up to us. "You've heard, Tomio?" Mr. O'Brien asked Dad.

He nodded, but the answer was already set deep into his face. "I have heard."

"It's war for sure," Mr. O'Brien said.

Mrs. O'Brien looked at Mom. "Oh, Michi," she sighed. "God bless us." She wrapped up Mom in a mother-bear of a hug.

Mom held on as if caught in a tornado. "Shame rains down on us," she murmured, and I remembered what she'd said about the double-edged sword. Those words had seemed far away; now they seemed too close. I felt chilled and hot at the same time.

"It isn't your shame, dear," Mrs. O'Brien said.

Mr. O'Brien offered his hand to Dad and Dad took it in both of his.

The O'Briens meant to comfort us. But then Mom and Mrs. O'Brien let go. Dad and Mr. O'Brien dropped their hands to their sides. Ray forced a sad smile. It felt as if something had died.

We left the O'Briens and trudged, voiceless, to our house, eyes ahead. But I sensed someone watching me. I looked into the nearest yard, where Mr. and Mrs. Richardson and their twin daughters—my age—stood and stared. Their arms were folded across their chests, their faces were ugly with hostility, their eyes flashed it in our direction.

I felt the shame my mother had spoken of. I felt anger at myself for feeling it. I had done nothing. But my dream day had suddenly turned into a nightmare. And what of the next day? What of my life?

I joined my family in our living room and heard the end of a news report. Sneak attack. Talks with the Japanese ambassador had given no hint. Thousands of innocent sailors feared dead. Declaration of war on Japan expected soon. Jap navy, Jap planes, Jap treachery, Jap this, Jap that.

Grandmother sat close to me on the davenport and listened. She spoke English with a thick accent, but she knew the language well. Dad had taught her, and she learned more from reading, her favorite pastime, and talking, her second favorite. She squeezed my hand.

Dad clicked off the radio. The room went silent. It was the silence that always hung in the air while they waited for me to leave. While they waited to begin their adult discussion. While they put on their long faces. I unraveled my fingers from Grandmother's and went to the entryway, where my coat hung on the coat tree.

I slipped it on slowly. I pawed through the cabinet for my

hat and gloves, pushing them aside, pretending to search while the murmuring began in the living room. I tugged on my gloves, checking my reflection as I passed the mirror. My face looked worried. It looked long.

"We're not the enemy," I heard Mike say. "Why do our neighbors glare at us?"

"Scapegoats," Dad said. "They are looking for someone to blame. We are the closest thing. In proximity. In looks."

"Not all of them are like that," Mom said.

Grandmother shook her head and uncorked a spout of Japanese, then English. The other voices joined hers in a jumble of words. I could feel the heat behind them.

They noticed me standing there. The talk stopped. I started for the door and like magic it began again. Just a hum, but I did pick out two words: Pearl Harbor.

The words meant nothing to me. But when I plucked them from the hushed conversation, like a prospector mines gold pebbles from a pan of swirling muck, my mind filled with wonder. I thought of *The Swiss Family Robinson* and *Treasure Island* and magazines with pictures of beautiful, faraway places. I imagined sunshine and crystal-blue water and brown girls diving from sturdy boats. I saw those girls descending through the water, down and down, to pluck oysters from the seabed, then rising like billowing jellyfish, lungs aching. I saw them prying open the rough and homely shells, finding a silky layer of rainbow-hued mother-of-pearl inside. And then, best of all, spilling from the open shells to their cupped hands: pearls. Pearls the size of marbles, glowing with light and color.

TWO

"Joseph," Mom called out as I reached for the doorknob. "Wait a moment, Joseph."

She walked into the entryway. She smiled and took her coat from the coat tree and slipped it on. "This house has grown stuffy," she said.

I pulled on my hat and we went outside. The air felt alive after the stillness of the house, after Dad's words. Did he really think our neighbors wouldn't like us because of what Japan had done? What did that have to do with us?

Our next-door neighbors, the Fujinagas, stood on their porch. All three—the mom, the dad, their little son, Timmy—waved to us and smiled thin smiles as we walked past. We waved back. I tried to smile. "Their house must also be stuffy," I said.

"Feelings sometimes grow too big to be kept within walls," Mom said.

I knew what she meant. The dark feelings in our house seemed to have taken over. I felt smothered by them. Out here I could breathe.

We crossed the road and neared the Langley place. Mr. and Mrs. Langley and their two boys—both in high school—were standing in their yard, staring up at the sky. I looked up, wondering what they saw. Nothing.

"Sneaky," I heard Mr. Langley say as we got closer. He saw us and raised his voice. "The treacherous Japs will wait till night, then pull another sneak attack."

Too late, I wished we hadn't crossed the road. I kept walking, not looking left or right. Mom moved between me and the Langleys. She took my hand and held it tight. Her hand felt damp. Out of the corner of my eye I saw the boys drifting closer. Then I heard someone spit, someone else laugh. A gob of saliva landed in the wet dirt three feet in front of us.

For an instant I waited for the dad or mom to say something to their sons, to make them apologize. I glanced at Mom, hoping she hadn't noticed, but her eyes were down, her face was flushed. At her feet was a rock, throwing-size. I bent and picked it up.

"Keep that stone in your hand, Joseph," she murmured, and tugged me on. My face was hot, my stomach knotted, my arm itched to rifle that rock at one of their heads. But I didn't. I held on to it, squeezing down, feeling its cool smoothness.

We kept walking, leaving our neighborhood behind us, leaving the hateful mutterings of the Langleys behind us. Yesterday I wasn't one of them, but I was accepted, I was a U.S. citizen, born and raised. Now I was a sneaky, treacherous Jap? My mother was someone to be spit at? It had taken less than five minutes to learn that Dad had been right.

"Your brother would have thrown that stone," Mom said. "Thank you for not doing so."

"I wanted to."

"That isn't the same. We need to show our neighbors who we are, that even if they're frightened, they don't need to be frightened of us."

We walked all the way to the river. At its edge I pitched my rock far out into the swirling middle. Then I sat on a big, mossy boulder with Mom, watching the water, swollen by rain, race past. Where would the river take me if a rowboat should magically appear on the grassy bank and I shoved off into the current? Pearl Harbor? The name felt like a ticket to a place I would rather be.

I picked up a fir cone and underhanded it into the water. Caught in a back eddy, it circled and dipped before sweeping into the mainstream and bobbing away like a cork on a fishing line. It disappeared, and I threw in a second cone, a third. I gave one to Mom and she tossed it in, but close, as if she didn't want to see it go, but it did. I watched it as long as I could, then let my imagination show me the rest of its journey. The river. The sound. The ocean. A faraway, warm-water, clear-water place of oysters and pearls and no war.

We went home. Almost. Our street, the in-town section of the road that led to Tacoma on the south and Seattle on the north, had been transformed. When we'd left for the river, it was empty. Now it was jam-packed. Now we had to wait as army cars and buses and jeeps and tanks and half-tracks and trucks pulling trailers with cannons and other pieces of equipment rolled past. Armed soldiers leaned from the trucks, stared out the backs, waved to the people standing along the street. Until they saw us.

We waited for a break, then ran across the road. Dad and

Grandmother and Mike were watching out our front window. They looked like prisoners.

We went in and joined them. We stood there for a long time, hypnotized by the blur of war machines.

"From Fort Lewis," Dad said. "Going to Seattle."

I nodded. "They waved to our neighbors," I said. "Not to us." I didn't mention the Langleys. Neither did Mom.

Mike spit some air through his teeth. Dad gave him a look. Mom left for the kitchen. Grandmother stayed, watching.

The kitchen table was quiet while we ate our rice and soup. Dad went upstairs and came back with two books. He gave one to me, one to Mike. They were the blank journals Dad gave to his English-language students at the Community Center, where he volunteered. I wondered why we were getting them. English was the only language we'd ever spoken.

"These promise to be interesting times," Dad said. "Not something we would wish for, but the times are already on us. I want you to remember them, to learn from them."

Mike set his journal on the table and folded his arms across his chest, as if he already knew what was coming.

"Your mother and I have taught you to observe what happens around you," Dad said. He looked at me. "Perhaps too well." I saw a smile in his eyes, and I knew what he was picturing: me hanging around doorways, listening for words that might matter to me. "You have learned to write in school and at home. Over the coming months, I would like you both to keep a record. For yourselves. For others if you wish."

"Every day?" Mike said, and I thought of our regular haiku lessons with Mom. While I looked forward to the writing, to the challenge of squeezing life-size images and big ideas into just a few words, Mike usually came to the kitchen table reluctantly. He would sit there, one eye on the clock, one eye on what was going on outside.

"Only when you have something to say," Dad told him, "which could be more often than you think. You and Joseph are citizens of this country, but you might not always be treated like citizens. The journals may give you an opportunity to express your feelings without inviting further trouble."

I expected Mike to complain. He had other things to think about: school, judo, basketball, friends. The coming war, his role in it. But he didn't gripe. He grinned. "Maybe I'll have Joe write mine for me."

Dad smiled, Mom smiled. Not for long, but it made my insides feel good. And I knew Mike was kidding, but I wouldn't have minded keeping a journal for him, too. I could make up interesting things to include, even if nothing interesting was happening. The writing would be good practice for me.

"No two people—even brothers—see things the same," Dad said.

Mike nodded. "I'll try it."

"Me, too," I said. The book felt good in my hand, solid. I imagined what I would write first. Something about pearls, maybe.

Someone knocked at the door. Mike answered. A moment later Ray walked into the kitchen. I jumped up, happy to see his grin.

"The stars are out," Ray said. He was dressed warm—thick wool coat, stocking hat, gloves. His dad's binoculars hung over his shoulder. "All of 'em. Wanna come out and look for shooters?"

I threw on my warm clothes and we headed for the door,

where we met Mr. and Mrs. Matsui on their way in. They had papers for Dad to interpret. I showed them to the kitchen and joined Ray outside.

We crossed the road to a vacant lot, away from the glare of lights. Our street and the yards bordering it were empty. People had no army vehicles to look at, they'd tired of talk. Ray spread out a burlap bag and we sat on it and craned our necks, looking for streaks of fire in the sky. The stars glowed blue. The sky was deep with them. I stared through the binoculars, imagining Japanese planes emerging from the black windows between the stars, showering down bombs. I felt a chill. Were the Langleys right?

"I saw the Langleys outside, looking for Japanese bombers," I said.

"Really?" Ray turned his face to the western sky.

"The Langleys thought they'd come at night."

"Dad told me don't worry," Ray said. "He said Japan's five thousand miles away."

"They bombed Hawaii."

"Hawaii's way closer to Japan." He was still staring at the horizon. "Dad said if they had aircraft carriers off our coast, they would've attacked us when they bombed Hawaii. Now they can't surprise us."

In the dark I couldn't see his face well enough to see if he believed what he was saying. Did his dad believe it? Did it matter if we were surprised? If a fleet of Japanese aircraft carriers showed up off our coast and launched a zillion bombers, could we do anything to stop them? It was my turn to search the horizon. "I hope he's right," I said.

"The Langleys are morons, anyway," Ray said. I didn't argue.

He spotted the first shooter. I was first to see the next one, a yellow-white slash that burned out in the sky over our roof. The moon came up, half full, and I peered through the binoculars at its giant craters. They reminded me again of the bombs, the war, what might be coming for Ray's family and mine.

Cold was seeping through my coat, up through the burlap and my jeans. I stood up, wondering what time it was, whether Dad, who believed in early-to-bed, was asleep. I wanted to tell him good night.

I noticed something. Far down the road, headlights—two pair—were headed our way in a hurry. Ray started toward the street, but I grabbed his arm and he stopped, following my gaze to the dancing lights.

The cars got within a block of us and slowed. I recognized the first one. It belonged to the chief of police. It pulled over in front of my house. The other car, a big, dark four-door sedan, stopped bumper-to-bumper behind it.

"What's *he* doing here?" Ray said.

The engines died. All I could hear was the sound of my heart, pounding in my ears. I could feel Ray's eyes.

The chief waited while two men got out of the second car. They were both taller than the chief. They wore long coats and big-brimmed fedoras like movie mobsters. But mobsters wouldn't be hanging out with the chief of police. What then? If not bad guys, what then? Good guys? Something told me that wasn't true, either.

They went to the door and rapped. The chief identified himself. Someone opened the door—Mike, I thought—and they pushed through. The door closed behind them.

"Come on," I said. We crossed the street. I couldn't decide if I should go inside. I didn't want Dad thinking I was putting my nose where it didn't belong.

The door opened. Dad came out, dressed only in his pajamas and robe and slippers. The men with hats towered over him on either side, clutching his arms, steering him, as if they were afraid he was going to run away, or faint.

They didn't know Dad. He walked on his own, head up. Behind him trailed the chief, Mom, Grandmother, Mike holding her arm. Mom's mouth was a straight-across line, but there were tears glistening in her eyes. Grandmother looked confused, Mike angry. What was happening?

Dad saw me. "Don't be afraid, Joseph," he said. One of the men shoved him into the back seat of the car while the other got behind the wheel. The doors slammed shut, the motor roared. The car made a squealing U-turn and accelerated back the way it had come.

"Sorry, Mrs. Hanada," the chief said as the taillights disappeared, the engine sound faded. "You don't argue with the FBI."

Mom said nothing. Had she argued inside the house? I wanted to think so, even though the chief said arguing was a waste of breath. Dad was worth an argument, no matter what.

She put one arm around me, one around Mike. Grandmother wandered to the edge of our yard and looked down the road, as if any minute the FBI guys would change their minds and bring back her son.

Ray hadn't moved since we'd come across the street. He stood in the shadows like a statue. "I should go," he said. His voice quavered.

"You don't have to," I said.

"I do," he said. "Sorry." About what? I wondered. What was he sorry about? He hurried into the night.

"Where are they taking Dad?" Mike asked.

"Don't know." The chief headed for his car.

I worked up my courage. "When will he come home?"

The chief got in his car. His engine howled to life and the car jumped, back wheels spinning, kicking up gravel and dirt. The tires grabbed, the back end ducked low, and the car fishtailed away.

Silence fell on us. Up and down the street, neighbors had returned to their yards, watching. They slipped into their houses.

"They should have let him get dressed," Mom murmured. "They should have."

Grandmother said something in Japanese, and Mom answered her, gently, in Japanese. Then, in English, "Come, Mother. Be with us." Like an uneasy bird, Grandmother settled next to me. We all stared at the empty road.

"Why did they take him?" Mike asked.

"Wrong man," Grandmother said. Her eyes glistened in the starlight.

Mom shook her head and sighed. "I have suspicions."

She led us inside. We sat on the davenport. "Your father is a leader in this community," she said. "It marked him." She went on, listing the stuff he'd done. I tried to pick out his crime. Dad taught judo and Japanese culture to our young people, but he also taught English and American business practices and interpreted contracts. He was an officer in the Japanese Association of Thomas, active in our church, in our schools' PTAs. "It is because of all this," Mom said, "that the FBI started watching him once relations with Japan began to crumble."

"You knew?" I said.

"Friends whispered in our ears," Mom said. "We knew. Especially after his trip to Japan last year. Even though he went only to visit aging relatives, not to set up a spy network or turn over secrets to the emperor, the trip attracted notice. It got his name on a list. And when the bombs fell, the names on that list were sunk, just like those faraway ships."

I thought about Dad leaving on his trip. He told me then not to be afraid, just as he did tonight, and he had come home safely. But I remembered the hours I spent at our living room window, watching for him to return. It seemed as if I'd waited a lifetime. How long would I wait for him now?

I took my journal up to my room and sat on my bed. I puzzled over what had happened, what I felt. I tried to imagine what was coming. Already our neighbors looked at us and saw Japs. My dad was gone, taken from his bed like a criminal. My country—the United States—was at war. Before long my brother could be fighting in it.

My head felt crammed, mostly with the memory of Dad, walking straight-backed, dressed only in his nightclothes, between the tall FBI agents in their wide-brimmed hats. The image filled me with sadness and pride. It almost made me smile.

He had told us to use the journals when we weren't being treated like citizens, when we wanted to express our feelings. He couldn't have known how soon that would happen.

Writing was often easy for me, and fun. I loved to let my ideas overflow into whirlpools of words that I could sort out on paper.

This writing would be different, though. This writing would not be easy, or fun. But I needed to try.

I thought of my day—perfect, then horrible—and the parts that mattered most. I struggled. I had words for what had happened, but not for what I was feeling. I forced images and thoughts onto the page until they finally began to come easier, to make sense. I ended with a haiku.

> *Pirates come at night,*
> *Seeking treasure—a man's dreams.*
> *He goes, still dreaming.*

THREE

Street sounds woke me to early-dawn darkness. In the bed next to mine, Mike slept restlessly, tossing and muttering. I crept to my window and saw headlights, the shapes of trucks and other vehicles streaming past our house like a long dirty river. Convoys. Soldiers. Going where? After Seattle, where? How many would return? Wrapped in blankets, I opened the window wide and sat in its chill, listening to the noises, watching until the last truck roared by and vanished.

There was no word of Dad.

I went to school. In some ways, it was the same. Mrs. Lynden said nothing about the bombing as we walked one by one into the familiar classroom that smelled of wet clothes and musty radiator heat and chalk dust. But I knew it was on her mind when she started the day with a prayer—a wish, she called it— for soldiers and sailors.

"May our young citizens, here in this school and everywhere in the land, be under Your care," she said, "and free of the fears and selfishness and prejudice that bring war, and that war brings."

We started our lesson—reading to ourselves—and Mrs. Lynden began a quiet journey around the room. She stopped at each of her young citizens—that's what she always called us— and talked softly and listened. I focused on my reader, trying not to overhear. Mrs. Lynden didn't think of me as an eavesdropper.

A row away and three desks toward the front of the room, Ray raised his arms in a big stretch. It was his signal that he was about to send me a message. I listened. In a moment the light tap-tap-tap of a pencil began, and I concentrated on the Morse code letters, then the words. A-L-L. F-O-R. O-N-E. All for one. I smiled to myself. It was the Three Musketeers' motto, which Ray and I had adopted for ourselves.

I raised my pencil and tapped back the answer. O-N-E. F-O-R. A-L-L. One for all. Ray turned and grinned, and the empty, aching feeling in my chest faded.

When Mrs. Lynden got to me, she crouched down and put her hand over mine and smiled, but her eyes looked sad. "Are you worried, Joseph?" she said.

I nodded.

"I'm sure your father will be home soon," she said. I felt my face get hot, my eyes watery. I wondered how she knew, until I saw Ray glance back at us. She had already talked to Ray. "Your mother and grandmother will take very good care of you until he returns," she continued. "And you have Mike." Her eyes smiled. Mike had been one of her students also, less interested in learn- ing but more outgoing than I was. I had heard Mom talk of him being a charming thorn in the side of his teachers. Would Mrs. Lynden smile at a memory of me in five years?

"They wouldn't even let him get dressed," I said.

"Raymond said it was scary."

"My father wasn't scared."

"Good," she said. "But there's nothing wrong with being scared. I think everyone's at least a little scared. Even the government."

"Where do you think they took him?"

"I don't know," she said. "But I'm sure he's safe. And warm. And missing you."

I nodded. I wanted to think so, too.

She smiled and got up and continued around the room. Wherever a kid was sitting in a desk, she stopped and talked, taking her time. But not all the desks were occupied. More than half of my classmates were Japanese American kids, and some of them were absent. I wondered if they were sick, or sick at heart. Had their dads been taken during the night? I thought of my friend Mae Mizuno, whose dad was in the Japanese Association with my dad.

Ray stuck close by me all day, and when he wasn't wearing his worried face he tried to smile, but some of the looks I got from the other white kids were different—cold glares, frowns, a quick glance and a quicker glance away. One, Lee Bogan, gave me a long stare, as if he were seeing me for the first time. The way the class divided up at recess was different: brown and white instead of swirls of both. Only Ray and I stood together, pretending things were the same. Around us there was more whispering, looking up at the sky.

When we came in from recess a piece of lined paper lay on my desk. I turned it over. Someone had drawn a picture of a grinning, toothy, squinty-eyed guy leaning out of an open-cockpit airplane. He held a bomb. Under the picture was my name, under that some fake Japanese writing.

I sat, my face growing hot, and crumpled the paper into a ball. Someone laughed. I looked across the room at Veronica Oliver, the only person in my class talented enough to draw that picture. Her face was pink, her eyes were turned away, she was fingering a shiny quarter. Somebody had put her up to it. I counted smiles. Five. Three boys, two girls—the Richardson twins. All of them had been my friends, or at least friendly to me, once.

I stood. My heart was pounding. My hands clenched and unclenched. The smile on the face of the closest of the three boys, Kenneth Stanley, faded as I took a step toward him. I hoped it wouldn't disappear. I wanted to smack it away. "You think this is funny, Kenny?" I said. I tried to keep my voice low, but it rose and trembled in my throat.

"I didn't—" he began.

"What is it, Joseph?" Mrs. Lynden said.

I stopped. "Nothing."

She studied me through the tops of her glasses. "If you say so." She watched me return to my desk, then started writing our lesson on the blackboard.

Her words blurred. I hunched over. So much had changed. But I hadn't. I was still a United States citizen. I had lived here my whole life. My parents had come here before the parents of some of my white classmates. Japan was the enemy, I wasn't.

I uncrumpled the wad of paper and smoothed it out on my desk. I blinked my eyes until they cleared, until I saw that what was written under my name was English, just made to look like Japanese characters. "The sneaky country where your parents were born attacked us," the words said. "Thousands of men are dead. Thousands more will die. Are you happy?"

Wiping at my eyes, I gazed around the room. No one looked back. I pictured myself in a mirror. To some, I had the face of the enemy.

But not to Ray. He walked me home. We talked about basketball. I didn't tell him about the drawing, the words.

Our car was still parked in the driveway. But in a different place? Dad had come home, I was almost sure. I burst through the door.

Mom stood just inside, hanging up her coat. Grandmother sat at the living room window. "We haven't heard anything, Joseph." Mom's voice was calm, but I could see worry in her eyes.

"Nothing?" I said.

She shook her head.

Mike barged in, his shirt torn and muddy, his face dark with anger. I hurried to close the door, half-afraid someone was on his tail. But he was alone, not talking. We followed him to the kitchen. He dropped his books on the table and went to the sink. He let the water flow over his knuckles. Mom went to him with a towel and soap. I saw blood.

"What happened, Michael?" She worked soap into his hands and rinsed them until he danced with pain. He didn't answer. He took the towel and dried himself. Pink flowers bloomed on the white cloth. Grandmother bustled around, bringing me milk and chocolate cake, making me sit.

"What happened?" Mom repeated.

Mike was mad, but he knew better than to ignore Mom. "Michael Hanada—the Jap—taught Earl Mueller some manners," Mike said.

"Sit," Mom said, and pointed to a chair. Mike sat next to me, eyeing my milk and cake. Grandmother brought him none. Mom brought him none. "What did you do?" she said.

"I planted his big farmer face in the mud." I heard pride in Mike's voice. I cringed. I had a feeling Mom wasn't in the mood for pride.

She sat across from him, eyes smoky. "He called you Jap?"

"Yes." The pride was gone. "And he pushed me. He kept pushing. Kids were there, outside the school. White faces everywhere."

"Will he be the last to call you Jap?"

"His parents are German immigrants. If they hadn't come here, he'd be marching with Hitler's Youth."

"Will he be the last?"

Mike shook his head. "No." It wasn't the answer I wanted to hear. I wanted to hear that it wouldn't happen again, ever. I wanted things back the way they were. I wanted Dad home. Suddenly I felt like a character inside one of the stories I had written—good guys, bad guys, bad stuff happening. I didn't like the feeling.

"Will you fight all of them?"

Mike took his time. His eyes sparked at the idea—fighting all of them. But finally he shook his head.

Mom gazed at him until he looked away, out at the darkening sky. "In our old country there is a saying, Michael. I think the leaders there have forgotten it, but they would have done well to remember."

Mike looked back at her as she put one small hand over his raw knuckles. "To lose is to win," she said. "Remember that, Michael." She put one soft hand on mine and stared at me until my face grew warm. "Joseph."

She got up and poured Mike a glass of milk. She cut him a piece of cake, gigantic. I didn't complain.

She turned on the radio. Music played. Someone knocked at the door. When I opened it, three families stood around our steps—Mr. and Mrs. Hoshida, Mr. and Mrs. Nagasawa, Mr. and Mrs. Yano. Their children, ten altogether.

"Come in," I said, not sure where they would fit.

Mr. Nagasawa shook his head. "Is your mother home, Joseph?"

"Mom!" I called. She hurried in from the living room. Mike and Grandmother came and stood next to me.

"Come in from the cold," Mom said.

Mr. Hoshida tipped his hat. "We can't stay, Michi," he said. He glanced over his shoulder, toward the street. "Tomio is not home yet?"

Mom shook her head.

"We share your loss," he said. "We pray for his quick return. In the meantime, we—all the community—will do whatever we can to help."

"Thank you," Mom said. But I knew her. She wouldn't ask for help. Still, it made me feel good to know there were people on our side.

"Please call on us, Michi," Mrs. Hoshida said. She smiled at us. "Your sons and mother-in-law, also." Grandmother held my elbow in her thin fingers. I felt them squeeze.

"We will," Mom said. "You are kind."

"He has done much for us," Mr. Nagasawa said. He and his family stepped back. "We will leave you to your evening." They turned and started for the street. The Hoshida and Yano families nodded good-bye to us and followed them. They got quietly into their cars and drove away. I wondered if we would see them again.

I had just gone back to the kitchen when there was another knock. This time Mike opened the door.

I arrived at the entryway in time to see Mr. Spooner walk in, dressed for church, or visiting. He was wearing a tie, he had his hat in his hands. His graying hair was slicked back from his thin face. I was used to him in overalls and a cowboy hat, working his farm or in town getting supplies. Dad leased our twenty acres of farmland from Mr. Spooner.

He nodded to Mom. "Mrs. Hanada." And to Grandmother. "Mrs. Hanada." He shook hands with Mike, then me. His hand was rough from fieldwork. "Boys."

"Mr. Spooner," Mom said. She closed the door behind him and the house went quiet.

"I heard the news," he said. "About Tomio."

"Yes," Mom said. "Would you like to come in?" She gestured toward the living room. "Have some tea with us?"

"I have to get back," Mr. Spooner said. "But I left a box next to your steps. From our cellar. Root crops, and things Mrs. Spooner canned."

"Thank you," Mom said. Her eyes looked wet. "But it wasn't necessary—"

"It's not much," Mr. Spooner continued, as if he'd memorized what he was going to say, "but you might have a need. And if there's anything more we can do, please come over, or send the boys, or call." He handed Mom a slip of paper with a phone number on it. She took it, but her eyes were down and she was swallowing, hard.

"Thank you," Grandmother said.

Mr. Spooner nodded to her, then Mom. "Boys," he said to us. He forced a smile and turned toward the door.

"We picked out a Christmas tree," I blurted out before he could leave. "From your land. A perfect one."

Mr. Spooner turned back. He smiled. This time it wasn't forced.

"It really is a perfect one," Mike said. "Joe found it on his own."

"No one asked for my opinion," Grandmother said.

Mr. Spooner blinked at her, as if he didn't know what to say to that complaint. "I hope you found the best one on the place," he said to us.

"We have it tagged," I said, hoping to keep anyone else from cutting it. "For after my dad gets home."

"I'm sure that will be soon, Joe," Mr. Spooner said.

"With a white handkerchief," I said.

Mr. Spooner chuckled. "That'll work," he said.

Mike opened the door for him and he walked out and down the steps. A veteran of the last big war, he usually walked like a soldier, but tonight his shoulders looked weighed down, his back bent.

It took both Mike and me to carry in the box and set it on the kitchen table, where Mom was lighting candles. Because of the fear of an air raid, the government had imposed a blackout. Electric lights were forbidden unless you had dark shades or black-painted windows or black paper covering them. We didn't have those things yet. It was scary walking around the darkening house, thinking about what might be coming through the sky. I reminded myself of what Ray's dad had said—if the bombers were coming, they would have already come. If they did come now, they couldn't see our candles from high in the clouds. Even the government said so.

I carried a thick stub of a candle to my room and watched as more convoys rolled past. I worked on my journal, finding myself writing more than I wanted, writing until the words captured what I had seen and felt.

Mom called me downstairs, into the living room, where she and Mike and Grandmother sat by the radio. Their faces looked spooky in the candlelight. An announcer was introducing a recording of a speech President Roosevelt had given that morning.

"Sit down, Joseph," Mom said, patting the davenport cushion between her and Grandmother. I sat. It felt good to be included, even though I had already heard about the speech.

The president's voice came on, sounding small. But his words were big. He spoke of the Japanese attack on Pearl Harbor, blasting away my visions of crystal water and pearls that shone like the moon. He said many lives had been lost, that military forces were severely damaged. He said the distance between Japan and Hawaii meant the attack had been planned for weeks, even as the Japanese ambassador was in Washington talking peace. The president reported the torpedoing of American ships on the high seas and attacks on Malaya, Hong Kong, Guam, the Philippine Islands, Wake Island, Midway Island. Familiar names. Unfamiliar names. My stomach twisted at the mention of each one.

The president asked Congress to declare that since the attack—unprovoked and dastardly, he called it—war has existed between the United States and Japan. And he said something else, something that prickled every inch of my skin. "Hostilities exist," he said. "There is no blinking at the fact that our people, our territory, and our interests are in grave danger." The words scared me; they made me think of invading armies, enemy ships off our shores, dive-bombing planes. But another thing bothered me more: I wondered if he meant me, my family, our community, when he said *our*.

FOUR

The next day at school was worse. Now we were officially at war with Japan. Some kids didn't know how to act around me, and that was okay. At least they hadn't made up their minds. Some had. They'd decided I was the enemy.

Mae came to school. Her dad was safe, so far, at least, she told me at recess. Her parents had just decided to keep her home the day before.

"There were some kids worried about you," I told her. I didn't tell her that one of them was me.

"My parents said they wanted me to hear the president's speech," she told me. "But I think they were afraid to send me to school."

I thought about Dad, locked away, not being able to hear the speech, and for a moment I envied Mae and her family. But then I pushed that thought back down to where it belonged. My misfortune wasn't Mae's doing.

"I heard about your father," she said. "He'll be home soon?"

"No one knows," I said.

She put her hand on my arm. I felt my face grow warm. "I'm sorry, Joseph," she said.

I hoped no one would leave a picture on her desk.

Other kids may have suddenly changed their feeling toward me, but Ray treated me the same as always. He wasn't the only white kid who did, but he was the one who counted the most. He was the one who kept the door open to what used to be.

We walked home in the rain—me hurrying, him hurrying to keep up. I had spent the day thinking of Dad, and I was eager to see if there was any word of him. But when we walked into the house, I knew there had been no news, at least nothing good. Mom was standing at the living room window, gazing out. She wore a sad-eyed smile when she saw me and Ray, and she spoke too quickly, before I had a chance to ask my question.

"What is the talk at school, boys?"

I shrugged. "The war."

"And?"

"Nobody's saying much," Ray said. "Just the morons."

"What do they say?" Mom asked Ray, but she was looking at me. She took our coats and waited.

"Some white kids give us looks," I said. "Even some who pretended to be our friends." I didn't tell her about the artwork they'd given me the day before, but part of me thought I should. I wanted her to know what it was like at school, but I wanted to shelter her from it also. "They don't talk to us unless they have to. Overnight, they changed. Or maybe everyone's just scared."

"Yeah," Ray said. "Scared. I am."

"Being afraid isn't a reason to turn on your neighbors," Mom said. "You haven't, Raymond."

It was Ray's turn to shrug. His face reddened.

"Have you heard anything?" I asked. "About Dad?"

She headed toward the kitchen and we followed her. Grandmother sat near the wood stove, darning socks. Thimbles on her fingers reflected light from the fire as she looked up and gave us a tired smile. Mom hung our wet coats on hangers and spaced them out on the wire that ran from the stovepipe to the wall.

"I tried," she said finally. "I called the authorities. The police chief knows nothing. The FBI will tell me nothing. I called a lawyer. The person I spoke to said the lawyer will call me back. He hasn't."

Grandmother shook her head. She looked small and, despite her dark, shining hair, older.

"Have they taken others?" I asked Mom.

"Mrs. Okura's cousin in Seattle. More, here in the valley, according to rumor."

"No one knows where?"

"No."

"What are the other families doing?" I said.

"I do not yet know who all the other families are," Mom said. "But I will find out somehow. I will ask if they have any information that would help us." She went to the counter and poured milk from a shiny glass bottle into a pan. "This may take time, Joseph."

Time? How slowly was time passing for Dad? How much time did he have? "There must be something we can do," I said.

"Government," Grandmother said. "The government is in charge now, Joseph. The government moves at its own pace. Your mother will do what she can, and I will help her. So will Michael. You can do your part by practicing patience."

And by staying out of it, as usual, I thought.

"Listen to the truth in your grandmother's words, Joseph," Mom said, and I decided to keep my mouth shut, at least for now. I would try to keep Grandmother's words in mind.

Mom put the pan on the stove. She got sugar and chocolate from the cupboard. I watched Ray's eyes light up. Ray thought Mom made the best cocoa in the world.

He called his mom to tell her where he was. We drank cocoa from big cups mounded with marshmallows. Mom and Grand-mother drank tea with milk and sugar. The kitchen was quiet except for the gentle sounds of sipping.

Ray and I went to the living room and turned on the radio. An Ovaltine commercial came on, and I knew I was tuned to the right station. It was time for one of my favorite radio programs. A gong signaled midnight, sending a little chill up my spine, then came the sound of a powerful airplane, far off, closer, closer, finally screaming into a dive. I felt my heart speed up. *Captain Midnight* was on the air!

Ray and I listened while Captain Midnight and his Secret Squadron tried to outwit the bad guys, Ivan Shark and his daughter Fury, but got into deeper and deeper trouble. Then another Ovaltine commercial came on.

"Not as good as your mom's," Ray said. He was right, but Mom's hot chocolate didn't come with a Secret Squadron Decoder.

The commercial ended. The program returned. Normally it would have had all my attention. I was a *Captain Midnight* fan, and I was also a writer. I hoped to someday write a *Captain Midnight* story good enough to be on the radio. But today I couldn't concentrate on the program. Especially a minute later, when it was interrupted with news of airplanes being spotted off our coast. I stared out the window, watching for planes, for Dad, for Mike.

The rain stopped. The sun, sinking, fanned rays of light through the overcast. Once more I pictured Japanese bombers, shooting out of the clouds like lightning bolts, diving down into our valley. I felt knotted up inside. I glanced at Ray, who was chewing his lip, twisting his long fingers together. I heard his knuckles crack. The news bulletin had ended, but *Captain Midnight* had never done this to him before.

Suddenly I heard the noise of a plane, loud and getting louder. I jumped to my feet, Ray jumped to his.

Then I realized it was the radio. *Captain Midnight* was after the bad guys, thundering after them in his eagle-winged racer. I relaxed. Ray smiled a sheepish smile. We cheered, pretending to ourselves that our Captain Midnight cheer, which we yelled out at least once during every episode, was what had gotten us up with our hearts pumping.

I sat back down, half-listening to the radio. Outside, Mrs. Jacobs walked by with her little girl, Emily. A week earlier they would have looked for me in the window and waved. Now their eyes were down, as if there were alligators in the grass. The Richardson girls skipped past, not looking left or right. Then Bobby Hatch and his cousin Mickey—guys I'd played basketball with—paraded by like royalty, noses in the air.

Captain Midnight ended. Ray had to leave. Mike came home, in a better mood. He let me practice some judo holds on him, then tried a few on me. He went to the kitchen for grown-up talk with Mom and Grandmother, leaving me flat on my back but wanting more. When I tired of hearing their murmuring, when I decided I wouldn't move closer to listen, I went to my room.

I flopped on my bed and stared at the spidery cracks in the ceiling. I imagined myself back downstairs. I'm at the table with Mom and Mike and Grandmother. They're all looking at me, waiting for me to answer questions about the war and how it's going to affect us. I give them brilliant opinions and they hang on every word. I stand up and pace around the room, gesturing and making keen observations and predictions, and they sit there in silence, sorry they hadn't included me in their discussions before.

I got up and put my ear to the cool wood of the floor to see if I could hear anything. But their voices were too soft, too far off. And no one called out for me to join them. I picked up my journal and moved my chair to the window and sat, looking out at the darkness creeping up on my town. I wrote about what I'd seen, about Dad. I added a poem.

> *Outside the window,*
> *Strangers—once friends—scurry past.*
> *Moles in black tunnels.*

Mike came up and sat on his bed. "Writing?"
I nodded.
He stretched out with his hands behind his head. "A story?"
"Journal stuff," I said. "You want yours?" It was at the foot of his bed, sitting on a handsome chest of drawers he'd made. As far as I knew, the journal had been there since he'd gotten it. Only two nights before. Why did it seem like two years?
"We're eating in five minutes," he said.

We ate, mostly in silence. I missed Dad's presence at the dinner table—the sounds of him being there—even though it meant him constantly questioning us, and Mike and I having to answer, to recount our school days and the progress of our studies.

I figured Mom, Mike, and Grandmother had already talked about everything important. Now it was the weather and Mrs. Kimura's new baby. I wanted to hear about the war, what it would mean to us.

"What about Germany?" I said finally.

"You have enough to worry about, Joseph," Mom said. "Germany is a continent and an ocean away."

"Japan's ally," Mike said.

"Vermin." Grandmother said it the same way she said *government*. She'd learned the word—*vermin*, not *government*—from a bottle of rat poison. "German vermin."

"Japan is our enemy," Mom said. "I am afraid Germany will also be."

"Nazis," Mike said. "The bullies won't bully us. They'll wish they hadn't picked this fight."

"We'll fight them, then?" I said. I pictured the war going on and on and me marching off to fight in it. I wondered how I would even get to the war. Or would it come to us, to our valley?

"With everything we've got," Mike said.

"Vermin," Grandmother repeated, louder, as if we'd been asleep the last time.

"Yes, Grandmother," Mike said. "Rats. Carriers of disease."

Grandmother nodded.

"It's what people are saying about Japan," Mom said. "About Japanese."

"We're Americans," Mike said.

"Nevertheless…" Mom said.

"Japan deserves whatever it gets," Mike said. "We don't."

Being in on the adult conversation wasn't what I'd pictured. They talked about bad things, scary things, but no one could tell me what was going to happen, no one asked for my opinions. I knew Mom didn't think I should be included. I went back upstairs. I didn't pick up my journal. What would I write? My fears? Mike wasn't afraid; I could see it on his face. That scared me, too. To lose is to win, Mom had said, but did Mike hear?

I looked out my window, down into the darkness of our front yard, and imagined Hitler, with his silly Charlie Chaplin mustache, his shiny boots, goose-stepping up our walk. I imagined Mike going out to challenge him, barehanded, smiling at his prospects. I closed my eyes, but the image wouldn't go away.

FIVE

Two days later, on December 11, 1941, Germany and Italy declared war on the United States. We had enemies across both oceans. How long would it take them to cross those wide blue highways?

The week ended, finally. I got home from school, glad to be away from the cool looks and cold shoulders. Mom and Grandmother and I were sitting in our kitchen when the telephone rang. I answered it, hoping Ray had come up with a good way for us to spend the weekend.

"Mrs. Hanada, please," a man's voice said. *Please,* but it was an order. He said our name like Canada instead of the way it was supposed to be pronounced, with soft *a*'s and the emphasis in the middle. He made our name sound like the squeak of chalk on a blackboard.

"Just a moment." I motioned Mom to the phone.

"Hello." She nodded. "This is Mrs. Hanada." She listened for a minute, then took a pad of paper and a pencil from the counter and sat in a chair by the phone and began writing. Mike came in. We all stared at Mom.

"He is okay?" she said finally. She lifted her eyes and smiled at us. I breathed deep and let it out.

"FBI?" Mike whispered.

"A mistake," Grandmother said. But she looked unsure.

"Not before then?" Mom said. Nodding. Nodding. "To where?" I tried to imagine the other half of her conversation.

She shook her head, not smiling anymore. "May I speak to him?" More nodding. "I will be there. Thank you."

She hung up the phone and we went to her, bombarding her with so many questions that she raised her hands, pulled herself away, and said, "Enough!"

She stood by the sink. We went to the table. She glanced at her notes. "He is in Seattle," she said. "And well, according to the man. I couldn't talk to him, but I can go to him on Monday."

"How long will he be there?" Mike said.

"Not long. A few weeks, maybe."

I felt a weight lifting. A few weeks. Not too bad.

"And then what?" Grandmother was frowning, as if she suspected something.

Mom looked away. "They are going to send him somewhere else. The man wouldn't say where."

"For how long?" I said.

"He wouldn't say."

Grandmother sighed, deep. The mistake wasn't being erased.

On Monday, while Mike and I were in school, Mrs. O'Brien drove Mom to a government building in south Seattle where they were holding Dad. When I last saw her that morning she was scurrying around, packing him clothes, shoes, a razor, and other things. She looked nervous, but color bloomed in her cheeks. I wanted more than anything to go with her.

By the time I got home that day, she was back. She and Grandmother were in the yard, pacing in the cold, talking.

"How is he?" I said.

She hugged me and smiled. "Whiskered. Thinner. But well."

"Did he ask about me?"

"All he spoke of was you and Michael and how much he
missed you."

My heart swelled until it felt heavy in my chest.

"Not of his ancient mother?" Grandmother pretended to be hurt.

Mom laughed. "He knows you are neither ancient nor easily
offended, Mother."

"What will they do with him?" I said.

"He doesn't know. Everything is secret. A man stayed in the
room with us. We weren't allowed to speak Japanese."

"It was good to see him?"

"Very good, Joseph." Her face was sad, but a smile crossed it.

Bittersweet. I thought I knew what the word meant. But knowing what something meant wasn't the same as feeling it. When
I saw the expression on Mom's face, I felt bittersweet. When I
watched Grandmother cling to every sad-happy word from Mom's
mouth, I felt bittersweet. Dad was alive, he was safe. But he should
have been free, not under someone's thumb. I waited for Grandmother to say government. Or vermin. But as Mom patiently
answered my questions, then Mike's a little later, the only sound
from Grandmother was a down-in-the-throat sighing, a prayer
for more sweet and less bitter.

Christmas crept up on us, and as it got closer, I found new worries.
Mom didn't drive; how would she be able to get our presents? How
would she be able to buy the battery-powered toy telegraph I'd

asked for? And if I didn't get it, how could I practice my Morse code? What about Mike's BB gun? And how about our tree? I imagined it standing proudly on Mr. Spooner's land, Dad's handkerchief dangling from its outstretched branch, fluttering in the breeze as if it were waving to us, beckoning to us to come and take it home.

Friday, December 19, was our last day of school before Christmas vacation began. It was also the day I had run out of patience. To ask about my presents would seem selfish, but I could ask about our tree.

I found Mom in the kitchen with Grandmother when I got home from school. A letter had arrived from Dad, and Grandmother was studying it. I looked over her shoulder at the messy piece of paper. There were nine lines of writing; four of them had been inked over.

"Who did this?" I said, trying to read what was left—*thanks for the clothes and shaving kit, miss you folks, doing okay, change in visiting days*—and imagining what was blacked out.

"Censors," Mom said.

"They muzzle him," Grandmother said. "But his voice is still with us."

"This doesn't tell us when he can come home," I said. "Or even if."

"He may not know," Grandmother said.

"He may not know where he is going, or when," Mom said. "But if he did try to tell us, the censors took care of it."

"Do they think we'll ride our horses after his car and jump aboard like cowboys?" I said.

"Maybe they have heard about Michael," Mom said, smiling, and Grandmother chuckled.

I found myself grinning at an image of Mike galloping after an FBI car, whooping and hollering and waving his Winchester. Or his BB gun.

I decided to get back to what had been on my mind. "When can we get our Christmas tree?" I asked.

Mom looked at Grandmother; Grandmother looked at Mom. "We may not be able to get your tree, Joseph," Mom said. "Not this year."

"This year is when we need it," I said.

"We don't have a way to get to Mr. Spooner's property," Mom said.

"We can ask someone," I said. "The Yanos, the Hoshidas, the Nagasawas—they all said they would help."

"They are all busy," Mom said, "and under much stress. And worried about being seen here. I do not want to ask them."

"Ray's parents would drive us to the tree," I said. "I know they would."

"Mrs. O'Brien has already driven me all the way to Seattle to see your father. She has promised to drive me again. I can't ask her for more."

"We could walk," I said. "Me and Mike could walk there, cut it down, and carry it home. Ray could help."

"Mike and I," she said, and I realized she wasn't volunteering to go, she was correcting my grammar.

"Mike and I."

"It's more than five miles to that property," she said. "After two hours you would arrive there tired. Then you would have to drag the tree home along the shoulders of busy roads. That would take twice as long, and there would be nothing left of the tree."

"We could—" I started to say we could carry it, but she raised her hand and lowered her eyebrows. The hand and the frown stopped me.

"It is too far, too hard, too dangerous."

"You and Michael could walk to the river," Grandmother said. "There are small trees there for the cutting. I could walk with you. I could give you my opinion."

I didn't want Grandmother's opinion. There were trees by the river, but they weren't *my* tree. "Maybe," I said.

I took my books and went upstairs to my room. I thought about continuing my story—a *Captain Midnight* story I'd been working on before the bombs fell. But the story wasn't so important now. And the idea of me getting something I'd written on the radio someday seemed like a little-kid pipe dream.

I wrote in my journal of a good month gone bad.

The next day, Saturday, Mom got Mike and me out of bed at the first sign of rainy daylight. She wanted us to clean out and straighten up the root cellar to make room for the stuff Mr. Spooner had given us. So after breakfast we headed outside, to the small, grassy hill that rose like a knob above the flat of the rest of our backyard. With Mike's help, Dad had tunneled into it and hollowed out a big enough space for shelves and walking-around room between the dirt of the floor and the low ceiling. We carried Mr. Spooner's box to the rear of the mound and down two steps, and opened up the big wooden door.

Inside, it smelled musty, like soil and things that grow under the soil. And it was cold. It seemed colder than outside. Mike lit the lantern and set it on a shelf so we could see once we closed the door.

I wasn't happy about starting my vacation like this. I could have been doing something fun with Ray, or listening to *Let's Pretend* on the radio, or curled up warm in my bed.

Neither of us said much as we went to work, moving boxes, rearranging jars of preserves, brushing away spiderwebs and the dead insects trapped in them. I'd told Mike the night before about our tree, and he wasn't any happier about it than I was. When I'd mentioned Grandmother's idea about going to the river to cut one, he shook his head. "Flood-stunted Tom Thumbs," he said. "Outside trees."

He closed the door against the rain, blowing sideways now. I felt the dark close in, even with the lantern lit. I was glad Mike was with me. I wondered what it would be like to be trapped in here alone. "Do you think Dad's in a place like this?" I said.

Mike leaned on his broom and looked at me. His eyes were dark holes in the weak, flickering light. "I bet Dad's place is warmer, Joe," he said. "And lighter. And bigger. But he can't open the door and go outside. He can't go home." I got a thick feeling in my throat.

We kept working, cleaning up and making space. Suddenly light flooded the little room. When I looked up, Mom stood at the open door, bareheaded in the rain, dark hair dancing around her face. A little smile tugged at the corners of her mouth, but she seemed to be tugging back.

"You boys have a visitor," she said, and for an instant my heart stalled. I thought maybe she meant Dad, that he was home after all, that she wanted us to see him for ourselves and be surprised. But in the next moment I knew it wasn't Dad. If it had been, Mom wouldn't have found it so easy to dim her smile.

"Who is it?" Mike said, moving for the door. Maybe he'd shared my hope.

"Follow me," she said, and we did, out into the blustery rain and through the back door. We took off our wet and dirty shoes and carried them to the front entryway, where Mr. Spooner stood, his rain-darkened cowboy hat in his hand. He looked like the Mr. Spooner I'd seen most often—work boots, work coat, overalls, striped shirt buttoned high. Everything looked wet.

He smiled. "Helping out your mom, are you, boys?"

"Joe's doing most of the work, Mr. Spooner," Mike said. "I'm doing the supervising."

I shook my head. Mike had done twice as much as I had.

"I doubt that, Mike," Mr. Spooner said. "I've seen you in the fields, remember."

Mike shrugged.

"Anyway," Mr. Spooner said, "it's nice to see you earning your keep. I asked your mom to go and fetch you because I wanted to show you something."

He opened the door and stepped outside. From the front porch he beckoned us to follow. Mike wedged on his shoes, but I slipped out ahead of him in my stocking feet. Instantly they were soaked and cold but I barely noticed.

There, leaning against the house, was a fir tree. A perfect fir tree. A white handkerchief hung from one branch. It was our tree, come home. Not Dad, but something good. Something *good*.

"Wow," Mike said. "I can't believe it."

I couldn't believe it, either. I couldn't help myself. I hugged Mr. Spooner and held on while he chuckled from so deep down in his chest, I could feel it come all the way through his wet coat. He hugged me back, then let me ease away.

"Thank you, Mr. Spooner," I said. "I thought we'd never see this tree again."

"Thanks," Mike said, shaking Mr. Spooner's hand.

"You're welcome, boys," Mr. Spooner said. "Glad to do it."

"You're very kind," Mom said from just inside the door.

Grandmother stood beside her, smiling and nodding at Mr. Spooner, but her smile seemed forced. I waited for her to say something about not getting to voice her opinion, but this time she held her tongue. She stepped outside where she could see the tree up close and eyed it, up and down. Her smile broadened. "It is a good tree," she said.

"A wonderful tree," Mom said.

Mr. Spooner put on his hat and pulled it low against the rain. I'd barely thought of the rain. He smiled one more time. "Merry Christmas, folks," he said, and started for his truck.

We called Merry Christmas and more thanks to him as he walked away, then stood on our porch and waved as he drove off.

Mike and I carried our tree to the backyard, where it would rest until Christmas Eve.

I studied the newspaper every day, even though the news—headlines that screamed of enemy planes over San Francisco, for instance—was often frightening. One day I waited for Mom and Grandmother to leave the kitchen, then picked up the paper—the Seattle Times—they'd been frowning and murmuring and shaking their heads over.

I read the story. The manager of Seattle's Pike Place Market was planning on asking the FBI if he could fire all the "Japs" who had stalls there.

I couldn't believe it. The guy wanted to sack everyone—U.S.-born citizens, or Nisei, and their Issei parents. He even wanted to get rid of the Japanese American farmers who supplied food to the merchants. Which meant trouble for our family and for many others in the White River Valley, where much of the market's produce was grown by people of Japanese descent.

Mom returned to the kitchen and found me glaring at the article. "The war has become an excuse for bigots to unwrap their prejudices," she said.

"Where will we sell the crops from our farm?" I said. "How will we live?"

"We don't know that this will happen, Joseph," she said. "If it does, we will find a way. We are the Hanadas. We are part of a larger family."

The words didn't comfort me. I wanted her to say that this was all a mistake, that nothing would happen, that Dad would come home soon and everything would return to the way it was. "We're Americans," I said.

"Yes," she said. "We are. Try not to worry."

I did try not to worry, but that seemed easier when I wasn't home. So whenever Ray invited me over, I went. His house was anxious, but my house felt empty. His house was still filled with his family; they faced the unknown together. Without Dad, we couldn't.

I thought about him all the time. I tried not to say much around Ray, because I didn't want to complain. But a few days before Christmas the rain stopped long enough for us to go out and shoot some baskets and he asked about Dad.

"We haven't heard anything new."

"Why do you think they took him?"

I remembered the reasons Mom had talked of, but they seemed too stupid to be true. I shrugged.

"Do you think they know something?" Ray said. "Something you don't know?" He turned his back to me and swished a shot.

I felt anger rise up, my face get hot. "What do you mean?"

"Maybe they had a reason. That's all I meant. My dad doesn't tell *me* everything."

"Their reasons are garbage," I said. My voice shook. "You want to play some one on one?"

"Sure," Ray said. He looked relieved that I wasn't mad.

"You take first outs," I said.

He took the ball back to our imaginary out-of-bounds line and dribbled it in. I attacked him like a swarm of wasps, darting in and chesting and shouldering and elbowing. I swiped at the ball but it was only an excuse to knock into him.

"What are you doin', Joe?" He backed me toward the basket.

I crashed into him. "Playing defense." I put a hand on his back. It left mud prints on his white undershirt.

Protecting the ball with his body, he crouched and leaned and came up, shouldering into my chest. I lurched back. He launched a shot. It missed. We both went for the rebound. I got there first but he had the height. He snared the ball, but that didn't stop me. I slammed into him and the ball bounced free and he let it go. I let it go. I charged into him. This time he was ready. He got his arms out and wrapped me up while I twisted and squirmed.

"What's wrong with you?" he grunted.

"Garbage," I said. "You're talking garbage." I freed an arm and swung at him and connected with the side of his head. I felt a surge of energy go through his body. He locked me up and wrestled me to the ground and rolled me on my back.

"That's enough," he said, working his way on top of me. He pinned my arms to the ground. "Knock it off."

I bucked and strained, picturing judo escapes. But he had me. "You're just like them." I tried to breathe, but his weight was on my chest.

"Who?"

"The FBI. The government."

"Just like them?"

"You think my dad's a traitor." But suddenly I wondered. Was it Ray's words that had made me mad, or was it that some part of me believed maybe they were true?

"I'm not like them," he said.

I felt tears in my eyes but I couldn't get my hands loose to wipe at them. They trickled, cool, down the sides of my face.

"I'm your friend, Joe. I just said the wrong thing. I'm sorry."

"Let me up," I said.

He got off and helped me to my feet. He was muddy, head to toe. So was I. He wiped at his face and left a smear of mud on his nose. He looked like a clown. I smiled. He smiled. "Morons," he said. "The government is a bunch of morons."

"I miss him," I said.

Christmas Eve arrived. It was different from other years, and not for the better. "I want to stay in bed," I told Mike when he woke me that morning. The gloom of war and what it was doing to our country, our valley, our family, weighed down on me.

Mike ripped away my covers. "Let's make the best of it, Joe," he said.

We did. After breakfast we brought in the tree. It looked bigger in the house, taller and fuller. Dew glistened on its dark green branches. Its smell filled my nose. Grandmother spent much thought and time directing us around the living room with it, finding just the right spot. She'd finally gotten to exercise her Christmas tree opinion, and she was milking the chance as if it were an overripe cow.

Mom carried in the box of decorations, then watched from the living room doorway, staying out of the decision-making except for an occasional frown, a grin, a raised eyebrow. We ended our search for the perfect spot on a raised eyebrow, but Grandmother wasn't paying attention.

"Perfect," she said. "Now for the trimmings."

We decorated, taking our time, hanging a string of lights, paper chains Mike and I had made in school, ornaments, tinsel. Finally Mike got up on a chair and clipped a silvery star to the tip of the tree.

"Plug in the lights, Joseph," Mom said.

I got down on my knees and scooted behind the tree and found the plug. With one eye on the branches and one on the wall socket, I slowly inserted the prongs, half-afraid the lights wouldn't work. And then what? No one in this room could fix them. The person who could fix them was locked away in a place where Christmas was just a wish.

The lights came on, different colors and shapes, brightening the green and shadows. Everyone looked, oohing and ahing, as I leaned back to admire our perfect tree. Then I unplugged the lights, imagining how they would look in the dark. I couldn't wait.

I had always had trouble sleeping the night before Christmas, and this year was no different, but it wasn't excitement alone that kept me awake on this Christmas Eve. It was sadness about what had happened, worry about what was happening, fear of what was still to come. When I woke in the morning, I was mostly tired, and lonesome for Dad.

There were presents under the tree, and many of them were mine. I opened the small ones first—comic books, new jeans, candy bars, books—*The Lone Ranger* and Dickens's *A Christmas Carol.* I saved the one bigger package for last, hoping.

Mike opened his biggest present and let out a whoop. He'd gotten his BB gun. My hopes rose. I ripped away the wrapping from mine, and there it was. My telegraph. I raced from the room, yelling out my thanks. I needed to call Ray.

Mom had been going to see Dad on visiting days, but she wouldn't be going again. She learned that he was being moved, somewhere out of state, somewhere far away. On December 27th, a Saturday, we Hanadas put on our warm clothes and walked to the nearest railroad crossing and waited. There was a rumor that the train carrying Dad and other men would be passing through our valley on its way to its destination.

People walked past. Cars passed. A freight train rumbled by. Cold seeped into my bones. Finally we heard a whistle in the distance. A train was coming. As it approached I could see it was carrying passenger cars, and I got ready to wave.

The engine roared past. Then the cars. I raised my hand. But the shades were drawn, top to bottom. Bars covered the windows. I waved anyway, just in case Dad was peeking out through a slit somewhere. We watched the train disappear. We heard its noise die away. Then we walked home.

Later that day I heard a report that the government would soon ask Japanese American families to surrender their radios, cameras, weapons, and anything else we could use to help Japan win the war.

Grandmother, who barely knew how to tune in a station, smiled bitterly at the story. She shook her head at the idea of us magically transforming our radio into a device for spying, of committing treason. "They see enemies where there are none," she said.

She added some Japanese words. Mom laughed, then translated for Mike and me: "Fear and ignorance give birth to absurdity."

Mike picked up a spoon from the table and held it to his mouth like a microphone. "Sneaky Mike Hanada to Japanese spy ship, come in," he said through his nose. He made staticky sounds through his teeth. "Come in, Japanese spy ship." More static. "Please tell your aircraft carriers that it's okay to bomb us now. The chief of police is having his afternoon coffee and doughnut, his gun is holstered, and the town of Thomas is completely defenseless."

I picked up another spoon. "Sneakier Joe Hanada to Japanese spy ship, do you read me?" I made my voice rise and fall, the way the radio sometimes did.

Smiling, Mom held an apple to her mouth. "Japanese spy ship here."

"The Hanada boys have decided to become traitors and spy for a country we've never seen before. So come and attack us. And while you're here, may we please have an extra helping of bombs?"

None of us was happy, but we all managed a laugh, even Grandmother. "Foolishness," she said, her eyes sparkling.

Our radio stayed in our living room.

SIX

January was nearly over when the Seattle newspapers began overflowing with bad feelings toward us. I read one article where the head of the state American Legion said all Issei should be sent to concentration camps. The next day a headline in the *Seattle Times* asked, KICK JAPS OUT OR KEEP 'EM WORKING? What would Dad say about these stories? Would he understand them? Could he explain them to me?

One day after school, I was sitting at my bedroom window when a big dark car pulled up and parked in front of our house. I got a bad feeling—a December 7th kind of feeling. I pictured Dad walking out to a car just like this one.

A tall man in a broad-brimmed hat and a long coat got out. He closed his door and leaned back, squinting up at our house. Then he opened up the car's back door and started fishing around for something.

I hopped up and headed downstairs on the run, two steps at a time. I found Mom and Grandmother in the kitchen. "FBI!" I said.

Mom jumped to her feet and peered out the kitchen window. Grandmother sat, shaking her head. "Not Tomio?" she said.

"No," Mom said, backing away from the window. "Trouble." She hurried from the room. "Joseph, answer the door, but not quickly!" she called back. I followed her as far as the entryway. She went to the living room while I faced the front door, my heart pounding. I heard her scurrying around in the living room, then hurrying past me, back toward the kitchen.

Someone knocked on the front door, loud. I stood, still as a statue. The back door opened, then closed. The knock came again, louder. Grandmother appeared at my side.

"Open it, Joseph," she whispered.

I waited another few loud heartbeats, then turned the knob and pulled the door open. Grandmother stepped in front of me to face the man. She said something to him in Japanese, loud.

"I'm FBI agent Herring, ma'am," the man said. "I'm here to survey your residence for contraband." For some reason he patted his briefcase. "This is the Tomio Hanada home, isn't it?"

"Con-tra-band?" Grandmother said haltingly, as if she'd never heard the word. She hadn't budged from her spot. Agent Herring still stood on the porch.

"Contraband," he said. He made a camera shape in front of his eyes. "Cameras." He put his hand to his ear. "Radios." He made a pistol shape with his hand, pointing his finger at Grandmother's chest. "Weapons."

"Ra-di-os," Grandmother said, and the agent looked past her to me, for help. I heard the back door close again. I heard Mom's footsteps in the kitchen. "Come in," I said.

Mom walked into the entry. Her face was flushed, but innocent. "Yes?" she said.

The FBI guy introduced himself and told Mom why he was there.

"We don't have those things," Mom said, and I glanced at Grandmother. Why was Mom saying this? Grandmother gave me a stern look that said Don't ask.

"I need to look anyway," Agent Herring said. "It shouldn't take long."

He went to the living room first. My chest suddenly felt empty. Mom and Grandmother stayed where they were, but I couldn't hold still. Curiosity pulled me to the living room doorway.

Agent Herring was walking slowly around the room, bending and poking and looking. While his back was turned, I peeked toward the radio.

It was gone. Our big Philco was gone. The table it sat on was still there, but now it supported a potted plant that up until five minutes earlier had sat on the living room floor.

Mom had snuck out our radio. I got more nervous. What would happen to her, to us, if it were found? Half of me wanted to smile, half wanted to throw up.

Mike, home from school, pushed through the door in a hurry. He'd seen the car. In a low murmur, Mom told him what was going on. His face darkened.

The FBI guy finished in the living room. He went to the dining room and pulled out drawers and pawed through dishes and napkins and stuff. He took Dad's long carving knife from a drawer and dropped it in his briefcase. "Contraband," he said with a scowl.

"It is a carving knife," Mom said.

The agent ignored her and moved to the kitchen. We watched

him go through drawers and cabinets. Two more knives went into his briefcase.

"What about the forks and spoons?" Mike said. "Aren't you going to take those?"

"I'm just doing my job, son," Agent Herring said.

He nosed around the rest of the downstairs, then went up. We went to the kitchen and sat. We could hear him walking around the upstairs, moving things, going from room to room, taking his time. Mom made us tea and gave us peanut butter cookies. I had to swallow extra hard to get them down.

"Why did they choose our house?" Mike said.

Mom shrugged. "Because of your father, perhaps."

"The notorious criminal," Grandmother said.

We heard footsteps on the stairs. The FBI guy came into the kitchen. He had a serious look on his face. I couldn't believe what he had in his hands. Mike's BB gun. My telegraph.

"I found these." He said it like an accusation.

"So?" Mike said.

Mom, standing, put her hand on his shoulder. "They are toys," she said.

"Not in my book," the agent said.

My face felt hot. My vision blurred over. This guy was going to take my best Christmas gift. "The telegraph," I said. "It doesn't do anything. It doesn't go anywhere. It just clicks. My friend Ray got one for Christmas, too. We practice our Morse code together."

Herring looked at me as if I were speaking Japanese. He dropped my toy into his deep briefcase. My heart sank with it.

"Ray's a Jap?" he said, flipping open a notebook, readying a pencil.

I shook my head. "A friend."

"Ray's just like you," Mike told him. "On the outside."

Agent Herring slipped his notebook in his coat pocket and gave Mike a tough-guy look. Mom's fingers whitened with pressure on Mike's shoulder.

"What's out there?" Herring said, nodding at the back door.

"Our backyard," Mom said. She swallowed.

"Any buildings?"

"No," Mom said, and my mind raced, trying to decide if she was telling the truth, or a lie on top of a lie. Could our little cave of a root cellar be called a building?

"I'll just take a look-see," Herring said. He walked over to the door and pulled it open.

I looked past him. We all did. In the late-afternoon dusk, the yard looked gray and featureless. The mound didn't look like a building. Not to me, anyway. What about to him? He was an FBI guy, but I knew he couldn't see through to the other side. He couldn't see the door.

He stepped down into the yard. He took another step, and another. He looked right and left. He stood there, so long I realized I wasn't breathing and my chest was beginning to hurt. I let out my breath and sucked it back in, quick but quiet. Mom turned away, trying to look unconcerned, but her eyes kept darting toward the back door.

He pivoted around and came back in and walked to his briefcase, sitting fat on the floor. He tilted it toward us so we could see inside. It was full of letters and Dad's papers and journals from the English Language School. And my telegraph.

"I found the papers upstairs," he said. He scribbled something on a piece of paper and gave it to Mom. "A receipt."

He grabbed Mike's BB gun. It looked silly in his big hand. He closed the briefcase and picked it up and walked out of the kitchen without another word. I heard the front door open and close, and a minute later a car door, an engine.

"Wait until dark, Michael," Mom said, "then go out to the root cellar. In the back, in Mr. Spooner's box, under the burlap, you will find our radio."

"Ra-di-o?" Grandmother said, her dark eyes twinkling. She smiled. Despite my stolen telegraph, I laughed. I breathed. It felt good.

February came. War hung over us like the gray skies that blanketed our valley.

"My mom speaks of 'the other shoe,'" I told Ray one day. "One shoe—the war with Japan—has fallen, she and Mike believe. They say soon the other shoe will drop."

We were at my living room window, listening to the radio. News of another victory by Japan. The fall of the Philippines, this time.

"What's that mean?" Ray said over the sound of the news-man's solemn voice. We still hadn't surrendered our radio to the government, and no one else had come to take it. They had taken my father. That was enough.

"I don't know," I said. "Something my dad hinted at in one of his letters. Something that will affect us—the Japanese Americans—because of the war." I stared out, watching for a familiar face in an unfamiliar car. Dad was locked away in a Montana detention camp now. There was almost no hope that he would be coming soon, but I spent many hours at that window. Hoping.

Ray shook his head. "I never heard my dad talk about another shoe."

"*Your* dad doesn't tell *you* everything," I reminded him.

The news guy droned on. "Where will Japan's victories stop?" he said. "Will they?"

People were frightened. And the newspapers kept feelings against Japanese Americans boiling. More articles—all bad—appeared. Stories of raids on Japanese American bad guys—spies—ran daily. I knew of no bad guys. No one did. But I noticed more bold-faced suspicion wherever I went—on the street, in stores, at school. Icy looks, cool whisperings. The word *Jap* followed me from place to place like a bad-tempered dog.

One day Mae was crying at her desk as I came in from recess. The back of her green dress was soaked with mud. "I fell," she told me when I asked her about it. I didn't believe her. I glanced up and down the rows, looking for a guilty face. All I saw was innocence, mocking me. I went to my desk, hands clenched into fists.

"What's the matter?" Ray asked. I couldn't answer him. He looked concerned, he looked as if he wanted to go on with more questions. But I gave him a frown. I turned away. I heard no more questions.

The next morning I made sure Ray and I arrived at school early, before any other kids. While he was in the bathroom, while Mrs. Lynden wasn't looking, I slipped a piece of paper into Mae's desk. On the paper I had written her name and a poem.

> *In a forest, dark,*
> *Sun breaks through, birds make music,*
> *Wounded hearts join in.*

Later, I watched nervously from behind as she found the paper and unfolded it. Her head bowed slightly as she read. Sunlight sifting in through the tall windows flickered off her dark hair, then flashed as her shoulders moved up and down in a sigh.

She turned. I lowered my eyes, but felt hers on me. My face warmed. I waited. When I finally peeked, she was again facing the front.

At recess I tried to act natural, not looking in her direction. But when I finally did, when I glanced across the school yard to where she was talking happily with her friends, our eyes met. She smiled, knowingly maybe. But her smile was worth her knowing.

Grandmother read the newspapers; she listened to the radio. "Like leaves," she said one day as I sat with her and heard the story of Singapore's surrender. "Countries are falling like leaves in the wake of a typhoon."

Would the typhoon come to our shores?

I sat with her on February 19th and listened to news of President Roosevelt signing something called Executive Order 9066. The announcer said the order authorized removal of people from certain areas of the country. Sensitive areas. West Coast areas. It transferred control of civilians in those places to the military. I looked at Grandmother's face. My stomach knotted. I thought of the other shoe. "What does this order mean for us?" I said.

"I don't know, Joseph," she said. "We will talk about it."

She may not have meant me when she said "we," but this time I wouldn't be left out. I wouldn't go to my room and imagine taking part in the conversation. This wasn't just rumors of far-off maybes. This was real. This was close.

When my family talked that night, I sat with them.

"Since I first heard of the order, I have talked to friends who have talked to other friends, Japanese and non-Japanese, some with ties to the government," Mom began. "The government," she said, glancing at Grandmother, "now has the right to move anyone living in certain areas away from their homes."

"That's what the man on the radio said." I wanted her to tell me something I didn't already know.

She smiled at me but it was one of Dad's children-should-be-seen-and-not-heard smiles. "The people who could be in trouble," she said, "are Japanese Americans living on the West Coast."

"Us," I said. This wasn't what I wanted her to tell me.

She nodded. Mike said something under his breath. Grandmother bit her lip. "The government is afraid we will turn our backs on America," Mom said. "That we will aid Japan—provide information, help with invasion plans, take up arms to fight against our own country."

This time Mike didn't pretend to call Japanese ships. He sat, unsmiling.

"They can't move us," I said. Could they? Where would we go? How would we get there? What about Dad? Would we be with him?

"Let them try it," Mike said.

"It doesn't mean they will," Mom said. "The people I have talked to—some in the Japanese American Citizens League—say it's only an option."

"They can't move us," Grandmother said. "Let them try it." She winked at me, then Mike.

Conversations cropped up everywhere. In our house, at school, in the homes of Japanese American friends, at church, in stores. People flocked together on street corners like pigeons, hunching their shoulders, bobbing their heads, cooing and gurgling.

One day I passed the Richardsons' house on my way back from Ray's. It was nearly dark, but I noticed the twins in their front yard, standing in the shadow of their big bare-limbed maple. I moved my eyes to the path ahead, pretending I didn't see their blond heads and Ivory soap faces and long heavy coats the color of blood.

One of them giggled, the sound of a horse's whinny. I should have walked faster, but I slowed, as if they were calling to me.

"Good-bye," one of them said, nearly pleasant.

I stopped and looked. Good-bye? They were smiling. "So long," the one named Wendy said.

I almost said good-bye. But I would see them again the next day at school. I said nothing.

"Farewell," Wanda said, louder, waving loose-wristed at me.

"Sayonara," Wendy said. She barely got the word out of her mouth before she burst into laughter, before Wanda joined her. Before I got it.

"I'm not going anywhere," I said, trying to sound sure of myself and brave at the same time. I felt neither.

I began moving toward home, but not fast enough. One of them recovered from her giggling and aimed another dagger at my back. "Have a nice trip," she said.

Rumors spread. Camps were rising in isolated areas away from the coast, where we would be taken. Where we wouldn't be a threat. The other shoe was falling. Still, I couldn't believe it would land on us. I thought of the stories from Europe—Jews and other "undesirables" taken from their homes, loaded onto trains, sent to camps. But that was Europe, that was the Nazis. This was America. It couldn't happen here.

But Mike sat down next to me on the davenport one evening, and I decided to ask him.

"It could happen." His words were like a fist to my chest. I looked across the room at Mom and Grandmother, expecting one of them to disagree. They sat in their chairs, saying nothing. "The army has the authority," Mike said. "And we can't afford to move to another state on our own. Not with Dad locked up and our bank account frozen."

"Our bank account?"

"Not just ours. All Issei accounts."

"'Let them try it,' you said."

"Yeah. I say things. But if we don't go to camp, we'll go to jail. Where would you rather go?"

"Neither one. I want to stay in our house. I want to stay in our valley with Ray and my other friends. I want Dad to come home."

"Forget it," Mike said. "You can forget about seeing him any-time soon. They've decided to send the rest of us away just because of how we look. With Dad, they think they have a real reason. They'll keep him until your whiskers turn gray."

Mom was listening to Mike's words. I wanted her to say he was wrong. I didn't even have whiskers. She said nothing.

Grandmother stood. She walked across the room and sat next to me. I felt her hand, soft, on the back of my neck.

"If they would let us show our loyalty," Mike said, "they'd see how much we care about this country. But they've taken that away from us too."

This wasn't the first time Mike had shown his anger over another new government decision—to change the military draft status of all Nisei men to 4-C. Unfit to serve.

When Mike had first complained, Mom pretended to be sympathetic. How could someone think her son wasn't good enough to serve his country?

"I would rather have you safe, Michael," she said now, dropping the make-believe. "Already many soldiers and sailors have died in battle."

"The government has done nothing for you," Grandmother told him. "Vermin," she muttered to herself.

"I wouldn't fight *for* the government," Mike said. "I would fight for our people. To *show* the government."

Grandmother said nothing. Mom said nothing. As long as Mike didn't have to fight, they would let him have his opinions.

Later, when Mom saw me at the window, she gave me a long, sad-eyed look. A he's-not-coming-home look. I didn't want to be the cause of her sadness. I went to my room, got out my marbles—cat's-eyes, swirls, aggies, puries, steelies, boulders— and lay a blanket on the wooden floor. I shot until my thumb throbbed. The click of glass sparked memories of dirt fields after a spring rain. I could smell them.

I found my journal, gathering dust beside my bed. My last entry was old—more than two months. Dad had said we wouldn't have something to record every day, but I'd had lots of experiences worth recording. I just couldn't make myself sit down to write, and when I did, the words wouldn't come. Some days I wondered if I was still a writer. It was as if some smelly, nightmarish creature was slithering around my room in the dark, making breathing noises, scaring me so much that I couldn't concentrate on any-thing but the smells and the sounds and what was going to happen next.

But this day I made up my mind to get something written. I went to my window and sat. I thought, and wrote about Dad, and President Roosevelt's order to move us, to set us aside like flawed marbles. I reworked the words until they said what I wanted, the way I wanted. I ended with a poem.

> *Hate whispers in his*
> *Ear: puries here, cat's-eyes there.*
> *He signs the Order.*

Newspaper headlines in the *American Star* and *Seattle Times* ex-ploded around us like Pearl Harbor bombs. STATE TO DISARM ALL JAPS. NEW RAIDS CONDUCTED IN SEATTLE. AREAS VITAL TO DEFENSE IN JAP HANDS. SEATTLE ALIENS TO GO. ARMY ORDER REVEALS EVENTUAL OUSTER OF ALL JAPS ON COAST. WHITES TRY TO BUY THEM OUT AT LOW PRICE. As March unfolded, I thought constantly of Mike's words, Mom's fears. I grew more and more afraid.

Ray and I walked to the river one afternoon. Winter was hang-ing on, but I saw signs of spring: green buds on trees, the sun riding higher in the sky, the river's swollen current. I pitched a rock and watched ripples swirl away.

"Was that your best throw?" Ray said.

"Left-handed," I lied.

"If you say so."

We chucked rocks into the brown water, testing our arms, testing each other. Baseball season was coming. Would I be here for it? Did they play baseball in Timbuktu or wherever I might go? Ray outdistanced me on every throw, but once we started going for accuracy, aiming for branches and debris heading downstream, I matched him.

Our arms grew tired. We sat on the grassy riverbank. "No talking about the war," Ray said.

"No talking about Nazis."

"No talking about the other shoe," he said.

"No."

"You think I'll make the basketball team at Oregon?" Ray said.

"Keep practicing," I said. "You'll be a star." What would I be?

A fighter plane flew over low. We looked up, silent. The war was nearly all we'd thought about for months; it was hard to talk about anything else.

The sun sank lower. "I think we're late," I said finally. We stood, turned our backs to the river, and began walking.

"Hey, kid!" The voice was belly-churning. It came from our left, out of a thick stand of firs. "Hey, O'Brien!" the voice called. Someone laughed, and two boys, high school age, skulked out of the trees like creatures from a scary fairy tale. We kept going at the same pace, although I wanted to hurry. I recognized one of them now: Earl Mueller. Ray's face was expressionless, but his eyes kept drifting off to the guys, closing in on us.

"Should we run?" he said without moving his lips.

"They'll catch us." Ray was big, I was fast, but these guys were five years older.

"Hey, Jap lover," Mueller said. The other kid giggled. Ray ignored them, we kept walking, but they giant-stepped to a spot ahead of us on the path and waited, chests out. We had no choice. We stopped, two strides away.

Mueller looked us over. He was big. His giggle-buddy was

bigger. "You're Hanada's little brother, right?" Mueller pronounced my name like the FBI guy on the phone—chalk-on-blackboard creepy.

"Yeah," I said, trying to sound dangerous. It came out squeaky.

"You a tough guy, too?"

I shrugged. There wasn't a good answer. Mueller's buddy giggled.

"You don't have Jap friends to play with?" Mueller asked me.

"A friend is a friend," I said.

"Yeah? You're gonna get this little friend in trouble," he said. "And you should know better," he said, glaring at Ray.

"A friend is a friend," Ray said.

"Vermin," I said under my breath but not far enough under.

"What?" Mueller's partner said. He did have a voice. He and Mueller closed the distance between us to a foot.

"Vermin," I repeated, hoping they were as stupid as they looked.

"What's that mean?" Mueller said.

"Japanese for friend," Ray said, and I fought back a smile.

"Yeah? How would *you* know?" sidekick said.

"You need to start hanging around your own kind," Mueller said to Ray.

"Joe *is* my kind," Ray said, and I thought he was being real brave until I saw where he was looking. Fifty feet up the path Mike was coming, walking fast. We *were* late, and he'd come to get us. I let go of my breath, and Mueller and his buddy must have sensed something. They turned.

Mike smiled, thin-lipped. "You're late, Joe," he said. "Your mom called, Ray. Dinnertime soon." He stopped six feet away, eyeing Mueller and buddy. "Everything okay?"

I could have said no, that the two trolls were up to no good, that they were threatening us and ready to do something worse. I had an idea that Mike wouldn't need much of an excuse to take them on, one against two, small against big, no matter. A piece of me wanted to see it; most of me didn't. "Everything's okay," I said, and Ray nodded.

"Good," Mike said. "Let's go."

We'd slipped past Mueller and friend, past Mike, when I heard Mueller say to our backs, "Before long you Japs will be where you belong."

"Keep walking," Mike said to us. We didn't. We turned as he faced the rats.

"If the government judged people by what's inside them," he said, "you'd be the ones going to camps. But we haven't left yet. Maybe we won't."

Mueller didn't say anything. His buddy stared at his shoes. We walked home in silence, with me hoping Mike was right.

He wasn't. On March 18th the government established the Relocation Authority, which would be responsible for carrying out Order 9066. Moving us wasn't an option anymore. It was decided. Our days in the White River Valley were numbered.

SEVEN

March wound down like a tired clock. I felt like a prisoner waiting to make his final request. I had one: Make Pearl Harbor just a bad dream. I could outlast a bad dream.

One drizzly afternoon I took a walk. I found myself at Mr. Spooner's place. In any other spring I would have been out there in the dirt with my family, working, planting. Not this spring. Our twenty acres lay untouched. I saw Mr. Spooner a hundred yards away, riding his tractor over his own section, plowing furrows in the black earth. He was alone.

Looking up, he saw me and climbed down. He walked to the road and shook my hand, not letting go. He pushed back his wet cowboy hat and the wrinkles around his eyes came out of shadow. He looked tired. "How you doin', Joe?" he said.

"Fine," I lied. "Where are your field hands, Mr. Spooner?"

He let go of my hand, waved out at the empty land. "I had some for a few days. Working hard, hoping. Then the relocation thing came out, and they thought, Why bother?"

"Sorry," I said.

"*I'm* sorry, Joe. How's your mom?"

"Strong," I said. "But she worries."

"No word on when you might see your dad?"

I shook my head.

"Remind her I'm here to help. If she's too proud, you come yourself."

"I will," I said. But I wouldn't. Pride didn't stop with my mom. Mr. Spooner shook my hand again. I watched him march back to his tractor and fire it up and begin plowing. I imagined Dad at the wheel of that tractor. I tried to imagine him where he was now. I thought about Mom, trying so hard to fill the empty space he had left behind. My heart ached at the same time it was swelling with pride.

I walked on. The fields should have been filled with people and activity. They were deserted. What was the point of planting? Who would care for the crops? Who would harvest? Young men were going to war, young women were going to Seattle to make bombers for Boeing. And Japanese American workers and tenant farmers? We were just going away. The abandoned farms were proof of that, even though part of me still didn't want to believe it.

A few days later the government found another way to make Japanese Americans feel like the enemy. We were put under curfew, which meant we had to be off the streets between eight at night and six in the morning. And travel restrictions. We could travel only five miles from our houses.

Curfew was hard. The first night I stood in my yard as white people walked or drove past. Then I went to my room and lay on my bed. I stared down at my old rag rug and imagined sitting on it, floating out my window. High above the yard and the street and the little people with their pale faces and pointy fingers. They reach up, trying to grab me, but I laugh and zoom away.

Having to stay closer to home wasn't as tough. Long walks weren't much fun anymore. I was tired of ugly looks and sharp words, worried about something worse. If I wanted to go to Ray's he came over and walked me back and forth. If I wanted to go anywhere else, Mike invited himself along. Mom made sure of it. He'd told her of our problem with Mueller and friend.

But one afternoon Ray and I decided to walk to town after school. It was the middle of May and warm and I was tired of the leash around my neck. As we neared the business area I noticed two soldiers nailing a piece of paper to a telephone pole.

We stopped and watched. They nailed another one below it. They stepped back and admired their work, then moved on to a pole down the street.

"What are they doing?" Ray said.

I didn't know, but my breath caught in my chest. A small crowd of white people was gathering around the soldiers, watching them tack up another poster. One man started clapping and cheering. He turned toward us, smiling. It was Mr. Langley.

"Shut up, Langley," a man's voice said from the back of the crowd. A familiar voice. The man pushed through to Mr. Langley and stared bullets at him. It was Mr. Davis, our school principal. "Go peddle your hate somewhere else."

They stood, facing each other, as voices rose, people took sides. Then the soldiers moved in, splitting up the crowd, herding them away. "Okay, folks," one said, "let's break this up. Let's move along."

"What's done is done," the other one said. "No sense making it worse."

People walked away, humming like bees. Some stayed to read the notices. Mr. Davis's wife took him by the elbow and led him off. Mr. Langley hung around, sharing a nasty laugh with his younger son, Harold. Across the street the policemen were taping other flyers to the barbershop window.

I hurried to the closest pole. Ray came up next to me and we stood side by side and studied the posters.

NOTICE, one said in big letters. HEADQUARTERS, WESTERN DEFENSE COMMAND AND FOURTH ARMY, it said under that. Farther down was the date, then the words CIVILIAN EXCLUSION ORDER NO. 79.

More words in smaller letters followed, but I skipped to the other paper. It was also from the Western Defense Command and Fourth Army. INSTRUCTIONS TO ALL PERSONS OF JAPANESE ANCESTRY, it said. The word *Japanese* was three times as big as the others, just in case we might have missed it. Or maybe they believed if we couldn't read English we could read BIG ENGLISH.

I thought I was ready for this. I had heard of other Japanese Americans already being taken away. Bainbridge Island and Seattle and just to the north of us in Kent and Renton. But I wasn't ready. A fog settled over me. Wet. Chilling. I breathed it in and it numbed my throat and when Ray asked me a question I couldn't answer. I just kept staring at the words.

Words that told of a Civil Control Station, set up at the Auburn High School gym, where a responsible member of our family, preferably the head of the family, had to report within two days for registration and instruction. Words that spoke of what the government would do to assist us in the "evacuation." Words that told us what we could take with us to our destination. An assembly center. Somewhere.

The list of what we could take was long—bedding and linens, toilet articles, extra clothing, essential personal items. But under the list was a warning that we could take only what we could carry. I pictured Grandmother, struggling with her belongings.

At the bottom of the instructions was the name of the army guy in charge of sending us away. Lieutenant General J. L. DeWitt.

I read the instructions again while Ray waited. I would have to go home and tell Mom and Mike and Grandmother about this. The government people wanted the head of our family to report to the Civil Control Station. But they'd already stolen away the head of our family. Now they were going to do the same to us.

My knees weakened from standing still too long, from the warmth, and Ray grabbed my arm and held on, keeping me on my feet. "Sorry, Joe," he said. "Let's walk."

We turned and took a few steps and almost stumbled into Mr. Langley and Harold. We stopped. They stopped. Harold eyed us, shaking his head sadly. "It's too bad," he said, looking at Ray.

"Yeah," Ray said.

"It's too bad you're only Jap on the inside, O'Brien, or we could send you off to summer camp with your little yellow buddy." His sad face broke into a wide grin. Ray charged him, but Mr. Langley stepped between them and held on to Ray.

"Let him come, Dad," Harold said, dancing around like a boxer. I would have loved to see him knocked on his back, but Ray would have been overmatched, even with anger on his side.

"You don't want to get your hands dirty, son," Mr. Langley said. "Head on home."

Harold quit dancing and moved on down the street. Mr.

Langley let Ray struggle loose, then turned and started after Harold. Ten feet away he looked back at me. "Pack your bag, son," he said. He grinned a muddy grin and continued on.

"Morons," Ray said, trying to catch his breath. He walked me home, then came in while I told my family. They seemed to take it better than I had. Maybe they'd already buried their last hope. Mom and Mike and Mr. and Mrs. Fujinaga walked back to town to see for themselves while Ray headed for home and I sat with Timmy Fujinaga and Grandmother.

"An adventure for you, Joseph," she said. "Something to write about."

"I would rather write nothing."

"That is your choice," she said. "But this wave will wash over us, whether or not you choose to describe it. To record your feelings."

I knew Grandmother was right. But something in me refused to admit it. I shrugged.

The job of being the responsible person in the family once again fell on Mom's shoulders. Grandmother was too old and cranky, Mike was too young and cranky, and I was just too young. And we'd all gotten more comfortable with Mom stepping in for Dad. So she went to Mike's school the next day and got instructions and tags for us and our stuff. In practically no time we were registered, numbered, and ready for shipment. As if we were cattle. All I needed was a brand on my behind.

They gave Mom our departure date—May 22nd, a Friday. Which meant we had five days to sell or store our belongings. The notice said the government would take care of some storage, but we had no reason to trust the government.

We didn't know where we were going, but Mom learned it

would be an assembly center, then a relocation camp. We knew that Japanese Americans from Seattle and other cities in Washington had gone to an assembly center at the Puyallup Fairgrounds. The government had named it Camp Harmony. Hah!

The O'Briens offered to store Mom's good dishes and our artwork, photos, and radio, and bought other things from us at a fair price. But the rest of the stuff we couldn't take was at the mercy of the scavengers who came to Japanese American homes looking for bargains, offering ten cents on the dollar, knowing we had little choice. Mom sold our Ford to a man for twenty dollars, our beds to another man for three dollars each.

A man came to our yard and spent a long time eyeing the chest of drawers Mike had spent so many hours crafting. Finally he offered Mike a dollar. Mike waited for the man to smile at his unfunny little joke. I smiled, then I didn't. The man wasn't joking.

"A dollar?" I said. Mike didn't say anything. He took a hammer from Dad's toolbox and smashed the chest to splinters. For a moment I stopped breathing. Seeing it destroyed tore away another piece of my life. But seeing Mike's pride in doing it brought chills to my spine.

"What will you give me for it now?" Mike said.

The man walked away, shaking his head.

"Vermin," Grandmother said.

There were many school days when the hands on the clock seemed frozen, when I couldn't wait to get out of my desk. But my last day of school went way too fast. I looked around the classroom in the morning, imagining it half-empty the following day, and the next thing I knew it was time to go.

Mrs. Lynden had been quiet. Whenever she began talking, her voice would get husky and she would stop and wipe at her eyes. "Choose something from your readers," she would say. "Or you may draw. Quietly."

No one gave me an ugly picture with my name on it.

"Line up, young citizens," Mrs. Lynden said now. We lined up, white and brown together, while she stood at the door. As we filed out, she stopped each of us who wouldn't return the next day and gave us a long hug. "Take care, Joseph," she said when it was my turn. Up close, she smelled like flowers. Her face was wet. She let go, and I was out the door. I didn't look back.

On the day we were to leave, Mike and I returned to the river. We lingered there, tossing a fir cone back and forth. Spring run-off had filled the riverbanks to their high-water marks. Seedling firs sprouted bright green needles. I touched them, breathing in their scent, locking it away in my memory.

When we got home, we went to our room and started packing. I saw Mike jam his journal in his duffel bag. But I had something for my journal, too much, a whole lifetime of memories.

I had little time to write, though. Mom called us downstairs to help. She and Grandmother were boxing things up for the O'Briens, covering the furniture with sheets. The radio played a familiar song. I had seen Mom and Dad dance to it when they thought I was elsewhere. She listened for a minute, then unplugged the radio and covered it with a tattered towel. No one talked. We stacked boxes in a corner. We could take only what we could carry in our arms and on our backs. We would not be taking much. Choosing had been hard for Mom.

Not so hard for me. I returned to my room and finished packing everything—clothes, comic books, marbles—except my journal. That I would carry. With my duffel at my feet, I sat one last time at my window and wrote.

Mom pulls the plug on
Glenn Miller's sweet moonlight song.
Echoes haunt the room.

Ray came over. He helped carry our bags to the front yard, where we sat while Mom and Mike and Grandmother did last-minute things inside. I wanted to be outside, where the air was fresh, where there were no walls. I wanted to experience open spaces for as long as I could.

"We've learned where they're sending us," I said to Ray.

He gave me a look—worried but trying not to show it, curious but afraid to ask.

"California," I said. "A place called Pinedale." When Mom had told us the name, I'd thought of log cabins, a lake, trees along its shores.

"Sounds okay, Joe," Ray said. His face said otherwise. "Kind of far away, though. I was hoping for somewhere closer. You know, a place we could visit."

"Yeah," I said. "A thousand miles is kind of far. Edge-of-the-earth far. I thought we'd end up at Camp Harmony first. Mom has a friend there."

Ray shook his head. "What a name. I'm surprised they didn't send you to Camp Co-op-er-a-tion." He stretched out the word like one of those long skinny balloons that circus clowns twist into shapes. Hats. Animals. Dive-bombers.

I looked up at the sky. "The *Post-Intelligencer* says sensible Japanese should be cheerful about this. That it's our patriotic duty."

"Start smiling," Ray said.

"They sleep in horse stalls at Camp Harmony," I said. "There are fences. Barbed wire." I took a deep breath and held it. Maybe if I didn't breathe, time would stop. I squeezed my eyes shut. Maybe if I closed my eyes, this would go away.

Neither one worked.

At two-thirty Mr. and Mrs. O'Brien drove up in their big Buick. Mrs. O'Brien and Henry went into the house to get my family. Trying to be cheerful, I helped Mr. O'Brien and Ray load duffels and boxes and Mom's and Grandmother's old suitcases. Everything we had fit with room to spare. We had packed our whole lives in the trunk of a Buick.

"Why don't you check on your mom, Ray," Mr. O'Brien said.

Ray didn't answer. He just climbed the steps and went in. When he returned, his mom and brother were with him. Behind them came Grandmother, then Mike, then Mom, taking one last look, making sure everything was put away, turned off, locked up. As if it mattered.

We crowded into the car, kids in back, adults in front. Luckily, Mom and Grandmother were as slender as the pickets of our fence. The back seat didn't bother me this time. I didn't want to see where we were going. I didn't want to get there first.

Mr. O'Brien started the car, but we sat there for a long moment. He was giving us a chance to take a last look. I rolled down my window for air and stared at the house. Its windows looked dull and empty, like the eyes of a dying trout.

On the other end of the seat, Mike leaned forward and looked, then slumped back. Next to him, Henry colored in a coloring book. Next to me, Ray reached in the pocket of his jeans and pulled out a small cloth sack.

"Before I forget." He handed it to me, and I knew what it was by its feel. I loosened the drawstring as Mr. O'Brien pulled away and I snuck one more look back. For what? Dad's familiar smile? I swallowed the lump in my throat. I turned the sack upside down and emptied its contents into my palm. Marbles. Six brand-new cat's-eyes, all different but all colorful and wide-eyed and smooth as butter.

"Thanks, Ray." I returned them to the sack and handed it to Mike.

"The red one's a little heavier than the rest," Ray said. "A good shooter."

Mike opened the sack and examined the marbles one by one. "Nice," he said. "The red one does have some weight." He gave them to me and I slipped the sack into the pocket of my jeans.

The conversation stopped, front seat, back seat. Outside it had started to rain. Big spring raindrops ticked against the roof as we moved slowly down the road, joining other cars in a sad caravan—hundreds of our neighbors leaving their homes behind, heading for the warehouse in Auburn where a train would be waiting.

I opened my journal, took a pencil from my jacket pocket, and began writing. Words came; more were forming in my head. But Ray was sneaking glances, and I felt myself getting carsick. I sat back and joined in the silence.

The loading dock outside the warehouse was crowded with people and luggage—two great mounds of it. We added ours, wondering if there would be enough room for all of it in the two baggage cars. It fit easily.

I saw many familiar faces—Japanese and non-Japanese. The Hoshida, Nagasawa, and Yano families stood together, waiting to board the train. Mrs. Lynden was there, dabbing at her red eyes with the sleeve of her dress. There were kids from school and church with their parents and grandparents.

Half of me was glad to see everyone, half of me was sad. While Mom and Grandmother were moving from group to group, while others were coming up to them and talking, while Ray was saying good-bye to other friends, I sat on a wooden vegetable box and took out my journal and continued writing.

It stopped raining, but the platform was wet and the air was chilly. It was time to leave. As I stood I felt a big hand on my shoulder. Mr. Spooner's hand. He had his cowboy hat pulled low. We shook hands while Mrs. Spooner clasped her fingers under her chin as if she were praying. She was dressed in her best church clothes. She smiled. Her heart wasn't in it.

"We said our good-byes to the rest of your family, but it was a little harder to track you down," Mr. Spooner said.

"You take it easy, Joe," Mrs. Spooner said.

"I will."

"We expect to see you back on the farm soon, Joe," Mr. Spooner said.

"It won't be the same without you," Mrs. Spooner said.

I couldn't answer. My heart tugged at my throat. Mr. Spooner let go of my hand and Mrs. Spooner took it in both of hers. "Godspeed," she said.

I found my family and the O'Briens. Mrs. O'Brien hugged all

of us, saving an extra-long, extra-tight one for me. Mr. O'Brien wrapped his arms around Mom and Grandmother at the same time, dwarfing them, then shook hands with Mike and me. Henry clung to my leg as I said good-bye to Ray. I started to shake hands with him, but he got me in a bone-crusher, lifting me off the ground with Henry still attached.

"Can we keep him?" Henry said. "Can we keep Joe?"

Mrs. O'Brien smiled, teary-eyed. "That would be wonderful for us, Henry," she said. "But his family would miss him so." And I would miss my family. But the government wouldn't have let me stay behind, anyway. I patted Henry on his bristly, crewcut head.

"Write me sometime," Ray said, reaching into his coat pocket. He took out two Hershey bars. "In case you and Mike get hungry."

I pocketed them in my jacket and said thanks while he pried Henry from my leg. We turned and walked to the train. Ahead of us, a soldier tried to help Grandmother up the steps. She pulled her arm away and gave him a frosty look and stepped straight-backed onto the train. I followed her, trying to keep my head up. My first train trip, but I wasn't excited; I was sick.

We found seats, Mom and Grandmother facing backward, Mike and I facing forward. Now I wanted to see where I was going.

We looked out the window. Many families were dragging out their good-byes. The O'Briens were just outside the window of our railroad car, talking to one another, glancing up at us, saying farewells to other Japanese American families. It felt good to see all the non-Japanese people. I had spent the last months imagining that most of them had turned against us.

As if reading my thoughts, Mike spoke up: "Look at all the white people who came to make sure we leave."

"Michael," Mom said. She gave him one of her darkest frowns. I handed him a Hershey bar to keep his mouth busy.

"From Ray," I said. "One of those white people."

He took the candy bar and held it up to the window. He gave Ray a thumbs-up, then opened the wrapper and took a big bite. "My favorite," he mumbled. "How'd he know?"

"He's your friend," I said.

Mike offered some to Grandmother, who shook her head. "Sugar," she said, and pointed to her shining white teeth. She was proud of the way they looked. Mom also said no, and I was tempted to eat mine while everyone was turning down offers to share. But I decided to wait. And while I waited, I had more to write. I wanted to write while home and the leaving were fresh in my mind.

> *The train stands chuffing,*
> *Awaiting its sad stragglers.*
> *All aboard, pilgrims!*

A soldier approached, stone-faced. Around his arm was a band of black cloth with the white letters MP. At his waist was a holstered pistol, dull gray, all business. Not the kind of silver, white-handled pistols Ray and I had worn while playing cowboys.

He looked us over, as if we were about to take out our radios and send signals to the Japanese navy, or steal some valuables, or escape. He gawked too long at Grandmother, and I was afraid she was going to say something, but she just stared through him, as if he were a dirty window.

Another soldier came by. He glanced at my journal and I thought he was going to tell me journals weren't allowed. But he smiled and nodded and moved on, head down. His eyes said he didn't want to be here, either.

Finally the chuffing got louder. I heard the sound of steam escaping, the squeal of metal against metal. With a small jerk, the train moved forward. It picked up speed, and I looked outside. The O'Briens were walking along with the train, smiling up at us, wet-eyed. Henry was waving. Around them were other faces, some trying to smile, some trying to keep from crying, some teary. All were white.

I waved one last time to Ray and his family as they ran out of room, as the train gathered momentum and its whistle blasted a long, unhappy warning. It was raining again. It kept raining as the train got out into open country, farmland and meadow and forest.

PART TWO

Desert sun beats down,

Kindling thoughts of home—cool rain,

Falling like teardrops.

EIGHT

Now our leaving home—the tearing away, Grandmother called it—was two months behind us. Now we'd left another place—Pinedale, California—but there was nothing bitter about this leaving. Pinedale Assembly Center was a place of burning wind and jagged barbed wire and three-inch-thick dust that rose in clouds and seeped in everywhere and clung to everything.

We'd made it through Pinedale because we didn't have a choice.

I hoped for something better as our train headed north, as the ramshackle car swayed and rattled and its wheels clicked like the keys of Dad's old typewriter. Across from me Mom stirred; her eyes fluttered and closed again. Mike sat next to her, head wedged against the window, eyes shut, breathing deep.

I couldn't sleep. It was too hot. July hot. Desert hot. The windows were half-open but the car was filled with other families and their breath and smells. The air streaming in from outside was thick with heat and dust and engine smoke. Sweat beaded on my forehead and ran down my neck and glued my shirt to the seat back.

But heat wasn't all that kept me awake. Excitement gnawed at my bones. We were moving. *We were moving.* To a place called Tule Lake. *Tule* rhymes with *coolie,* Mike had noticed. I decided it couldn't be as hot there, at least, and maybe there would be trees and green fields and water. And friendly faces. Pinedale had none of those. Pinedale had baked dirt and barracks and guard towers manned by grim-faced soldiers.

I looked at Mom. Her face was filled with worry. She looked older, with new lines around her eyes and darkness under them.

Mike, too, had aged. A few months earlier he'd been a kid like me, just bigger. Now his face wore hollows and shadows, his body had stretched out. His threadbare pant legs rode high above his ankles.

I looked out the window: flat brown desert, scrubby bushes, cloudless pale sky. Far overhead the sun beat down.

Above the western horizon dark shapes emerged, speeding toward us. Fighter planes, flying low. As they got closer, they took on the form of a V. I looked for markings, feeling my heart thud against my chest, staring until my eyes hurt. Then I saw the U.S. insignias—the circled stars—on the undersides of the wings and let out my breath. I'd seen planes like these in one of the dog-eared magazines—*Life* or *Look,* probably—they'd brought to us at Pinedale. Wildcats. I liked the tough name: Don't cross my path.

The planes roared overhead and continued on, but my heart still raced. I couldn't forget the newspaper photos of death and destruction I'd seen in December. I couldn't get rid of the picture

I'd formed in my own mind: Japanese bombers racing in low over Diamond Head toward Pearl Harbor, where U.S. warships, caught off-guard, lay at anchor.

Around me little kids chattered and squirmed, older kids and adults slept or stared out windows or spoke in hushed voices, while I thought of those bombers. Grandmother sat a few seats away, talking with friends. I could hear her soft, musical words rising and falling in that faraway language of hers. But I thought of those bombers, what they had done. *What they had started.*

Mike stirred again, then Mom. But sleep held them. A soldier ambled up the aisle. He was tall, blond-headed. A perfect Nazi. But he didn't walk past, unseeing, as many of the soldiers did. His eyes danced; he smiled as he looked from person to person. He stopped and talked to a young mom whose baby was fussing. He took a handkerchief from his pocket and gave it to her and she wiped at the shoulder of her worn dress, where the baby had spit up. He patted the baby's head and smiled and moved on, leaving his handkerchief with the woman.

As he got nearer, I looked down at my lap, at my journal. I hadn't written anything in it since we'd left home, but I thought maybe now I'd feel more like it. Once we got closer to the new place.

He stopped next to my seat. I looked up.

"Doing some writing, Mr. Twain?" he said quietly, eyeing my sleeping mother and brother.

Mr. Twain. Mark Twain. I'd read his stories. I'd seen the movie *Tom Sawyer.* But I wasn't Mark Twain. "My name's Joe Hanada."

The soldier—a sergeant, I noticed—stuck out his hand. For a second I hesitated; I thought he wanted something from me—

my journal, maybe—but then I woke up. I reached out and watched as my hand disappeared in his, leaving only my wrist and the tip of my thumb visible. It was like shaking hands with a baseball glove. His grip was easy but I had a feeling he could crush every bone if he chose to bear down.

"Sandy," he said. "Like the stuff under your feet. Like Orphan Annie's dog." He laughed, gently. "Sandy Farrow. But you can just call me Sandy."

Not sergeant? Not sir? He held on to my hand as people around us looked. "Nice to meet you," I said, and he let go. I waited for him to move on. I wasn't used to talking to soldiers. What would the people around me think?

"I'm not a writer," he said. "But I'd like to be. Before the war I was a teacher—kids your age—when I wasn't surfing."

Surfing. I'd seen pictures somewhere. Men riding flat, bullet-shaped boards on giant waves.

"Great American novel?" he said, sitting down next to me, glancing at my writing.

I smelled Old Spice. Dad's smell. I felt eyes on us. "Just a journal."

"Good idea," he said. "You'll want to remember this."

"It was my dad's idea."

"He's not here?"

I studied his face. His eyes were alive with warmth—Mr. Spooner's eyes, only younger. I imagined this soldier—Sandy—in twenty years, graying but still straight-backed. "Fort Missoula. In Montana."

He nodded. "Oh. Sorry."

"Maybe he'll join us at Tule Lake," I said.

He nodded again, then took another look at my journal. He faked a serious, FBI kind of expression. "So you've got spy stuff in there?"

I smiled. I remembered sitting at our kitchen table, playing spy. I remembered listening to the radio with Ray, day after day, decoding messages, tapping out our own on our telegraphs. "Secret code," I said. "For *Captain Midnight*."

He grinned. "Ovaltine," he said. "My wife's favorite. She grew up on it."

"You have a wife?"

"Hallie. Beautiful as you can imagine. Inside and out. Teaches school in San Diego."

Hallie. "I like her name."

"Beautiful, isn't it? Just like her. It's Greek. It means 'Thinking of the sea.'"

"She should try my mom's hot chocolate," I said. "My friend Ray says it's the best."

Mom moved in her sleep and Sandy lowered his voice. "I wish she could," he said, peering out at the brown land slipping by.

"I apologize for the looks of this country," he said after a while. "You should see the real California. In San Diego the hills are green, the weather's comfortable, the beaches go on forever, and the ocean—the warm, blue ocean—rolls in, wave after wave after wave. Like the best dream you ever had that keeps coming back again and again and again."

He might not have been a writer, but he talked like one. A travel writer, maybe. But mostly he talked like a friend. Like I was someone he was happy to spend time with.

"I've never been to California—that one, anyway."

"You'll have to, Joe." He glanced around the car. "After this is over." We shook hands. "I'll see you again, Mr. Twain."

"Okay." He moved on, talking to others, but not as long as he'd talked to me. Part of me was relieved to see him leave, to feel the attention of onlookers fall away from my shoulders. Part of me wished he would stay.

I opened my journal and read, hoping for inspiration, a running start. I had thoughts, but they weren't translating themselves into words.

Mike opened his eyes and sat up. He stretched, every muscle. His clothes looked even smaller. I was glad he'd been asleep when Sandy stopped. He would've been polite but cold. I would've found it embarrassing.

"Beautiful scenery out there," Mike said, eyeing the dead countryside.

"It's not the real California."

"How would you know?"

"I've heard of a beautiful California," I said. "Trees, oceans, beaches."

"You heard that Pinedale would be a pleasant place. It was a nightmare. You heard that Tule Lake will be like a resort. We'll see."

Mom woke up. When she saw where she was, her eyes went flat. I felt a chill. In the deep desert heat, I felt a chill. I remembered what Dad had said about our Christmas tree—how it would begin dying as soon as it no longer had its roots. Was something dying inside her?

She unfolded her hands. In them was a rumpled letter from Dad, zebra-striped by censors. We still didn't know when we would see him. She wrote to him often but his letters to us were rare and lifeless. He knew the government would analyze each word, and anything spirited or suspicious would be inked over or sliced away.

She patted Mike on his knee, me on mine, and stood. Her eyes looked more alive. "I am going to walk about," she said, "to visit friends." She had friends, which was good. Some from our old home, some she had met at Pinedale who were making the trip to Tule Lake. Fellow pilgrims.

When I was boarding this train I'd seen kids I knew from the White River Valley. From a distance, I'd seen a girl who looked like Mae, but I couldn't be sure and I didn't have time to investigate. I hadn't seen Mae during our time at Pinedale. The two friends I'd made there, the Miyake brothers, weren't being assigned to Tule Lake.

I sensed someone standing next to me; I sensed a uniform and Old Spice. I looked up. Sandy was back.

"Hungry?" he asked me. Mike was concentrating on the landscape. "I'm Sandy Farrow," he said, loud enough that Mike couldn't ignore him. He stepped between the seats and held out his hand to Mike, who finally looked up. They shook. Mike's hand, bigger than mine, disappeared in Sandy's cave of flesh.

"Hungry?" Sandy repeated. He held out two Hershey bars, and I took one.

"Thanks," I said.

Mike shook his head. "I don't eat Hershey bars." Then he remembered his manners. Or maybe he thought Mom was lurking nearby. "Thanks, anyway."

"You're welcome, uh, big brother."

"Mike."

"You're welcome, Mike." He offered me the other bar. "For later, Joe?"

I took it. There was no such thing as too many Hershey bars. "Thanks."

"Sure." He continued down the aisle. "You young citizens take it easy." Young citizens. I hadn't heard that expression since my last day at school. I got a lump in my throat, too big to think about eating. I set the Hershey bars on the seat.

"Why'd you lie to Sandy?" I asked Mike.

"*Sandy*, is it? He looked like the police to me."

"He's okay."

"We don't need to take candy from guys like that, like poor immigrants. We *are* citizens."

With one swipe he scooped up the Hershey bars and cocked his arm. His hand flashed toward the open window and suddenly they were airborne, soaring out over the desert. I imagined them instantly turning to goo in the scorching sun.

"Why'd you do that?" I said. "They were just candy bars. And they were mine."

"We'll get our own candy," he said.

"Vermin," I said. I kept my eyes ahead, thinking of the taste of that chocolate. I opened my journal. Now I had something to write. Thoughts. Feelings. I waited for words. They came slowly, as I tried to find the right ones to mourn my lost candy, to sum up two months of feeling like an outcast, of living like an exile. I tried to figure out what to say about Sandy, the guard who seemed like a friend. Why did it feel that way? I thought of Ray and his family and Mr. and Mrs. Spooner and Mrs. Lynden. Because Sandy *was* a friend, I decided. Or he could be.

I looked up. Mike was staring out the window again. "Sandy isn't the enemy," I said.

"Sorry, Joe," Mike said. "*You* should be the big brother." He smiled, but kept his eyes on the landscape. I looked, too, almost hypnotized by the barely changing colors: brown, then deeper brown, then lighter. At the horizon, sky and earth looked the same: dirty tan, lifeless.

I wrote for a while, then closed my eyes, out of words. Pinedale had made me soft. I was good for a few lines, then I felt lazy and empty and I had to rest and do the thing I'd learned to do best: nothing. Breathe in, breathe out. Nothing.

A shadow fell over us. Sandy was back. "Mind if I sit?"

"No." But Mike was another story. I looked at him, waiting to be embarrassed.

"Mike?" Sandy said.

Mike tore his gaze away from the landscape. "Sure," he said.

Sandy sat next to him, not giving him much room. Mike inched closer to the window.

"I have a rule against giving advice when none's been asked for," Sandy said to Mike. "But I'm going to break my rule, because I don't think you'll ever ask."

I half-expected Mike to get up and leave, but he sat. He tugged at his pant legs.

"You deserve to be angry," Sandy said. "Joe does, all your family. But you've got a tough path to walk. That anger is going to weigh you down, wear you down, keep you from seeing the possibilities, the difference between friend and foe."

He stopped, but Mike didn't say anything.

"You understand what I'm saying?"

"I understand," Mike said. "But if you were in my shoes?"

"I'd be just as angry. But I'd hope someone would talk to me, make my path gentler." He looked at Mike's battered, dusty shoes, then his own boots—shiny, nearly new, as big as platters. "And I think my feet would hurt," he said. He smiled, and Mike gave him a half-grin. More than I expected.

Sandy looked at me. "Joe?"

I nodded.

"Good. But I'll be hanging around, just to make sure."

"At Tule Lake?" Mike said.

"For a while."

I watched Mike's face. The half-grin came back as Sandy stood.

"Still don't like Hershey bars?" he said to Mike. He took two more from a paper sack.

Mike shook his head.

"For you then, Mr. Twain." Sandy handed them to me. "Maybe you'll get to eat these." He winked at Mike, whose face reddened. Then he walked away.

When Grandmother returned, I told her about Sandy and what had happened. I told her she could call me Mark Twain.

NINE

We arrived at the train station at dusk. Klamath Falls, Oregon. Still hot. Red sky to the west. But there were trees. And mountains. My hopes climbed. As we boarded buses, I wondered how far we were from the camp. I sat in a front seat; I wanted to be the first to see our new home.

Others seemed eager, too. As our bus growled and groaned through the city streets and onto the highway, their voices rose above the noise.

By the time the bus slowed, it was dark. We had left the trees and mountains and recrossed the border to California. A faint glow hung over low hills. Everyone's eyes were on what lay outside; in the murk it was mostly imagined. All I saw as we turned left off the road was what the bus's headlights picked out. A paved driveway, scrub bushes on either side, and as we got farther along, a sign: TULE LAKE WAR RELOCATION CENTER.

The driveway turned right. The driver stopped the bus and opened the door. A guy in a uniform and a flat-brimmed hat stepped on, looked down the aisle, then stepped off again. "Go ahead," he grunted and the bus moved forward, through an open gate. Ghostly lights shone down from up high.

The bus hushed. My heart fluttered and froze. What I could see sickened me. Barbed-wire fences strung between guard towers. Hulking, raw-wood, tarpaper-covered buildings I recognized as barracks. Knots of soldiers and other uniformed men glaring at the buses as if they carried the plague. And parched soil in every direction. Not paradise. Pinedale all over again.

Home. This was home.

I looked behind me for Mike, Mom, and Grandmother. I knew they were back there, but in the gloom they were invisible.

The bus stopped in a large space of dirt. Other buses pulled up next to ours. Soldiers met each one. I sat, waiting for my family. Then I stood and followed them off into the night.

We milled around, collected our luggage, listened to instructions, stood in snaky lines. Mike and I waited while Mom and Grandmother were questioned and fingerprinted like criminals. Mom forced a smile at us as a man pressed her fingers onto a pad of ink, but I could see the shine of tears in her eyes. My chest ached. When it was Grandmother's turn, she stood with her chin up, not watching.

Everyone looked lost, betrayed, and in the unearthly lights, half-dead. I thought of a movie Mike and I had seen. It was about this ancient dead guy who came back to life and wandered through the night under the control of some evil power.

"Remember *The Mummy's Hand*, Mike?" I asked him.

"Scary," he said.

"Look around you."

Mike studied the crowd. He put his arms out in front of him, half-closed his eyes, half-opened his mouth, and began stumbling around in a small, ragged circle. I laughed. Other kids laughed. Mom and Grandmother and other adults didn't. They seemed puzzled. And maybe nervous about what the guys in uniform would think.

But when Mike stopped his act, the uniforms didn't seem to notice. They were busy processing other mummies, getting us ready to march off to our barracks.

We walked for a long time, weighed down with our belongings. The place was huge. Low building after low building, guard tower after guard tower, miles of barbed wire, armed sentries spaced along it, eyeing us. And dust I could taste. A fog rolled in and hung in the air, and I imagined I was in London, seeking shelter from the rain of German bombs. But dirt caked on the soles of my shoes. I wasn't in London.

At last we arrived at our barracks. The building was squat and homely and smelled of new wood and tarpaper. We were assigned to a small room—an apartment, they called it—on one end of the building. We walked in. There were four bunk beds spaced across the wood floor. Nothing else. No bed for Dad. I wondered if these people knew something.

"Cozy," Mike said.

I paced it off with my short legs. "Eight by ten," I said. About the size of our living room at home. Overhead there was one bare bulb. It cast our shadows on the floor, the bunks, the thin wood walls that separated us from the next room.

"Inches?" Mike said.

"Funny," I said. "Paces."

"We can live here," Mom said. "Perhaps we can get some furniture."

"A table," Grandmother said. "Some chairs. It will be okay."

Okay? It didn't feel okay. Their words felt like frosting on a cake made of sawdust and sand. But it was an improvement over Pinedale. At Pinedale, our room had grown so hot that the metal legs of our bunks sank into the asphalt floor. At Pinedale, spaces between the roof and outside walls allowed bugs the size of birds to swarm and creep into our room. Inside walls had been ceiling height but there was no ceiling, only rafters and the roof far overhead. The family next door could hear everything we said and did, and we could hear them. At times, when the parents were away and the voices of their two boys rose like sirens, Mike would pull himself up on the wall and glare at them until quiet returned.

We took bedding and a few other things from our bags and boxes, found the building that housed the bathrooms, and came back to undress for bed. Mom reached up to turn off the light. Darkness would provide our only privacy. She wouldn't complain, but I saw sadness on her face, and loneliness, and shame.

I lay down and stared up into the blackness, listening to noises in our room and from elsewhere in the barracks.

I awoke to daylight. Mike was in his bunk, asleep, but Mom and Grandmother were gone. I tried to guess the time. Before seven? The sun seemed low, the air was still cool. I dressed and sat on my bunk and took out my journal. I wrote of our new home, trying to be like Mom and Grandmother and say something positive. I managed only a few lines and a poem.

Tule beginnings—
Stone-faced soldiers, guns, barbed wire.
Hearts full of wishes.

When I returned the journal to my duffel bag, my hand
brushed against my sack of marbles. I'd taken them out only
once at Pinedale, after Mike had agreed to brave the sun.
Outside, the target marbles almost disappeared in the powdery
dust. We tried shooting, but the shooters dug in and vanished. A
wind gusted up, blasting dirt into our eyes, turning the air
brown, and suddenly I couldn't see any of my marbles. They were
buried. We sifted through the dust until we found all but one,
and we called it quits.

When Mom and Grandmother returned—from visiting, they
said—we went to breakfast at a mess hall where the people
from several barracks—called a block—ate. I mostly pushed my
food—canned sardines, powdered eggs, oatmeal mush—around
my tray, the same as I'd done at Pinedale. But Mike ate big. He
was growing.

We were leaving the mess hall when I heard someone call my
name. I turned to see a kid running to catch up, smiling. Phillip
Yatsuda, from Thomas. He was a year behind me in school, and
one of the kids I'd known at Pinedale.

"Did you just get here, Joe?" he said, falling in step, breathing
hard.

"Last night," I said.

"We've been here a week," he said. "Better than Pinedale, huh?"
Still smiling. Always.

"Much," I said.

"I can't wait to see the swimming pool," Mike said.

"There isn't—" Phillip began, then glanced at Mike's face, caught his joke. "There's a canteen, though." His smile widened. "Lots of stuff to buy."

"If we had any money," I said.

The smile dimmed just a little, then returned. "There's a school," he said, "and a hospital, and a cemetery."

"Three strikes," Mike said. "We're out."

"A cemetery?" I said. How long did they expect us to be here? Who would want to be buried in this place?

"Is that where they get the teachers?" Mike said. "The cemetery?" He started his mummy routine again, stumbling around in the dirt outside the mess hall. Mom and Grandmother hurried on.

Phillip laughed. "We'll see," he said. "School doesn't start for a while."

"That's the first good thing you've said," I told him. I missed *my* school, but I didn't think I was ready for school taught by zombies inside barbed-wire fences.

"You guys want me to show you around?" Phillip said.

"Sure," Mike said, and we called good-bye to Mom and Grandmother. Phillip told his mom and dad what he was going to do. His mom smiled at us. Phillip's smile. His dad looked us over and nodded. His face was frozen in a scowl.

Phillip proved to be a good guide for someone who'd been at Tule Lake only a week. We followed the fence—not too close, Phillip warned—around much of the camp. He showed us the canteen, the post office, the schools, the hospital, the jail, the cemetery. At Pinedale there'd been nothing much to look at outside the fences, but here there were hills. Some even had names: Castle Rock, with its spires reaching into the sky; Mount Abalone, with a necklace of rock that gave it its other name: Horse Collar Mountain. They were brown and bare, but farther away were other hills with a few trees, and in the distance rose a snow-capped peak.

"Mount Shasta," Phillip said. "Looks close, but they say it's fifty or sixty miles as the crow flies."

"Or the buzzard," Mike said

I imagined walking to it, hiking through the trees at its base, splashing through its cool streams. I thought of Mount Rainier near our home, how it had hidden itself in clouds the day we left. I longed to see it again.

Phillip returned us to the mess hall. In two hours we'd seen most of what there was. He pointed out his barracks—just two away from ours—and said he should get back.

"Thanks for the tour," Mike said. "But we didn't get to see the pool."

"But you did see the cemetery." Phillip left us with his smile attached.

There was no place we had to be until after lunch, when new-comers were to assemble in the mess hall and listen to a wel-coming speech. Mike returned to our barracks, where he could escape the sun. I decided not to follow him. I'd just seen a girl emerge from a neighboring barracks and melt into a crowd of kids. She looked familiar. She looked like Mae. I approached the crowd with hope in my heart.

I couldn't see her. Maybe I'd been mistaken. I counted half a dozen girls her size. Maybe one was the girl I'd seen.

I skirted around the swarm, then took a deep breath and plunged in, smiling as if I belonged. Some of the kids smiled back, some of them looked familiar—from Pinedale, maybe.

"Joseph?" The voice rose above the others.

I turned, and there she stood. "Hi," I said. Now that I'd found her, what was I going to say? "Mae," I added. Somewhere between my brain and throat rose a dam. Then, finally, "I thought it was you."

"It's me." She smiled and came close. I forgot about the crowd. "How are you?"

I wanted to tell her not good, but better now that I'd found her. My mouth wouldn't make those words. "Fine," I managed. She kept her smile glowing, her eyes on me, waiting for something. "And you?" I said. My everyday manners had grown rusty in two months.

"Better now that I've seen you," she said. "I thought I saw you once at Pinedale, but you were far off, walking with your brother. My mother told me not to shout."

"You should have," I said. "Two months in the same camp, and I never saw you."

"There were many people," she said. "These are some of them." She gestured—a sweep of her arm.

"Five thousand there," I said. "A city."

"Fifteen thousand here, my father says."

I whistled. "Three cities." I hadn't forgotten my arithmetic.

"Can you teach me to do that?"

"What?"

"Whistle. If I had known how to whistle, I could have gotten your attention at Pinedale."

"Your mother would have approved of you whistling at me?" I felt myself smiling at the image.

Her laugh sprang from her chest, musical. "You're right. But I'd like to know how."

"I'll teach you."

We talked for a long time, but it didn't seem like it. Her family was staying in the barracks next to ours. We made plans to meet in the afternoon.

After lunch, an army officer spoke to us, fast and with some kind of accent. I was full and sleepy, and what he said was aimed at the adults and went over my head like one of the small birds that had found their way into the building. I paid more attention to the birds than to the man, but one thing he said didn't escape me: We—the Japanese Americans—were at Tule Lake for our own protection. I was a kid, but I knew that wasn't true. Any of us would have loved to take our chances outside those barbed-wire fences.

I looked at Mike, whose face was stony. Mom squeezed my hand. Grandmother sucked in a quick gulp of air, as if someone had just pushed her into a cold river. She let it out in a long, low hiss.

I wondered if Dad was also being held for his protection. Maybe in my next letter to him I would ask, and see if the censors would let him answer.

Once again there was nothing for us to do. I returned to the barracks and sat down on my bunk with my journal. The air was heavy with heat. I remained as still as possible, but sweat oozed from my skin. My hands were wet with it, and I had to wipe them on my thinning pant legs to keep my journal dry as I sat and fingered the pages.

Mom and Grandmother came in. Grandmother sat next to me and nodded at my journal. "Mark Twain," she said. Her eyes twinkled. Without peeking, she watched as I began to write, as I struggled. I squeezed out a few sentences. I envied Mark Twain, his way with words.

I closed the journal. I needed to get outside. I needed some air with life in it.

"Your father would be proud," Grandmother said. She smiled, showing off her perfect teeth.

"Thank you, Grandmother," I said. But I wasn't writing for my father. I was writing for myself.

TEN

I stepped outside the door and was nearly blinded by the brightness of the day. A figure, tall and uniformed, approached from out of the sunlight.

"Joe," Sandy said. "I was coming to see how you folks are doing."

"Okay. Hot." I turned. Mike was coming, walking with a guy about his age.

"Remember James Ito?" Mike said to me.

I nodded, but I wouldn't have remembered his name.

"James was at Auburn High with me, and at Pinedale but on the other side of the camp. This is my brother, Joe." He looked at Sandy. "And Sergeant Farrow."

James Ito offered me his hand. "Joe," he said, and we shook.

"Sandy," Sandy said. He reached out and swallowed up James's hand and made James's eyes widen.

"Nice to meet you," James said. Then to Mike: "See you after supper." He went into a room in our barracks. Mike and I had both found nearby friends and suddenly things didn't look quite so bleak.

"What did you think of the captain's talk?" Sandy asked Mike.

"He didn't fool anybody," Mike said. I found myself nodding.

"My thoughts exactly," Sandy said. "But whatever the reasons you're here, you have to get through this, right?"

"Right," Mike said.

"Good." Sandy squinted up at the sun. "I can't do anything about the heat. But I've got something that might help you tolerate it for a bit." He shrugged an army-green canvas pack from his shoulder. Water dripped from its bottom onto the ground, making little dust puffs. The side of his shirt was wet. He unsnapped the pack and held it out to Mike. For a moment I was afraid he was going to shake his head no, that whatever it was— more Hershey bars, a pound of gold, pearls—he didn't want any. But he reached in and took out a shiny-wet bottle of Coke. His smile gave away his feelings.

"Joe?" Sandy said. I didn't hesitate. I plunged my hand through chunks of ice and wrapped my fingers around the neck of a bottle. I wanted to just keep feeling that icy cold. But I wanted a drink more. I pulled out the bottle and held it against my cheek. Sandy smiled. He got out the last one for himself, then pried off the caps with the bottle-opener blade of his pocket knife. We drank.

Nothing ever tasted as good. Kids walked by, giving us the eye, and maybe I should have felt stingy. I didn't. Someday they'd get their own Coke specially delivered in a sack of ice. Maybe. Today it was my turn, and I wanted it to last. But in this heat it wouldn't. So I downed the Coke, I thanked Sandy, Mike thanked

Sandy. He told us to keep our chins up, and then he returned the bottles to his pack and said good-bye.

Cooled off, Mike and I walked. When we got back to our room, Mom had a surprise for us: photographs of Dad, of our family, pinned to the wall that separated us from the next room. I hadn't seen them since we'd left home. She hadn't put them up at Pinedale because we didn't know how long we'd stay. It made me feel good to see them, but it also made me sad. I could see Dad but I couldn't. And having those pictures on the wall meant we were here for a long, long time.

Later that afternoon I met Mae outside her barracks. We sat on the ground where the building made shade.

"Phillip Yatsuda's here," I said.

"Is he still smiling?"

"He'd smile at the devil."

She laughed. "Reverend Sakamoto says the devil may retire soon. That there are enough other people doing his work."

"He's here?"

She grinned. "The devil?"

"Reverend Sakamoto." I'd seen him once at Pinedale. Before that he'd been at St. Paul's, our home church.

"Yes," she said. "Will I see you at church?"

"I don't know," I said. "Since my dad's been gone, no one seems interested."

"Not your mother or grandmother?"

"I think we're all waiting for a sign—an answer to our prayers."

"Your father is still safe?"

"Yes."

"Maybe that's your answer."

"To one prayer, yes. But we're still praying for his return."

"He'll come back," she said. "I know he will."

I wanted to ask her when, but I knew that was an answer she didn't have.

"I miss Mrs. Lynden," Mae said after a while. "Hearing her call us young citizens."

"Me, too," I said. "I miss school, the writing."

"You're a good writer," she said. "I remember the Thanksgiving play, your poetry—the haiku."

I recalled reading one of my poems out loud in Mrs. Lynden's room. I remembered my nerves and the knot in my throat more than I did the haiku. But was Mae talking about that poem, or another one—the one she had found in her desk? I studied her face: Her eyes were down, but she smiled a shy smile; her skin colored.

"I'm keeping a journal now," I said, moving on. "It was my dad's idea."

"A good idea," she said. "My dad writes letters and mails them to my mother."

"But they're both here."

"Yes," she said, as if such a strange thing didn't need an explanation.

I gave her what I hoped was a quizzical—not stupid—look.

"He was in Japan when I was a baby," she said. "He wrote beautiful letters to my mom. She saved them. When he returned, she made him promise to keep writing to her once a week. So he has. He still puts them in the mail, as if he were far away. She still saves them. I guess it's their own way of keeping a journal."

"I miss my dad," I said.

"What do you hear from him?"

"Not much," I said. "He's had hearings to decide what will happen to him, but nothing's been decided. He's lonely but he tries not to let on. He tries not to worry us, so he doesn't say a lot. Then some of what he says gets inked over or cut out by censors. But my mom has taught us to pick out thoughts from between the lines. And sometimes we play a game, making up foolish, crazy things to take the place of the missing words."

Mae grinned. She listened. It was good to have someone besides Sandy to talk to. My family preferred not to talk, to me at least; I was still the baby.

Mae and I discussed the war, what each of us knew. She too had heard of Nazi concentration camps and torture and death.

"President Roosevelt called *these* places concentration camps," Mae said, looking around.

"I wouldn't trade places with the people in Nazi camps," I said. "But I would trade places with President Roosevelt. I'd like to see him live here for a while."

"I would give him my straw mattress," she said.

"And he could have my sardines."

We laughed. The day was ending better than it had begun.

"The Japanese—they also have done bad things," Mae said.

"Pearl Harbor." I remembered how I'd once heard those words and seen images of paradise. Now all I saw were the real pictures— ships resting on the harbor bottom, thousands of men trapped belowdecks.

"And now Bataan," she said. "The Death March. Thousands of American soldiers dead. Civilians slaughtered."

I'd heard of Bataan, a peninsula in the Philippine Islands, and what the Japanese had done to our soldiers. Once, before we left Pinedale, Mike and Mom had talked of it late, after the light was out, after Grandmother's breathing grew slow and even and I made mine sound the same.

"It wasn't us," I said. "We're Americans. We're citizens."

"I know that," Mae said. "But we're here. We're judged by what they do."

I nodded. I knew it was true.

Mae returned to her room, I went to mine. I felt as if I'd walked into an oven, as if a fire roared in the little stove. Even with the windows open there was little movement of air. But Mom had another surprise. There had been letters waiting for us, and she had them now. One from the O'Briens, one from Dad.

She handed them to me. "Your grandmother and Michael already read them."

Mike and Grandmother were gone, driven out by the heat. But I sat on the floor, back to the wall, and it seemed a little cooler. I expected Mom to go out, too, to get some air, but she stayed, pacing, watching me but pretending not to. Why?

I opened the O'Briens' letter first, saving Dad's. Mrs. O'Brien had written the main part of the letter. She wrote about war news, crops, weather, shortages, rationing, people we knew. It all seemed far away.

Ray wrote the last part. He didn't have much to say, or maybe he didn't say much because he didn't want to make me feel bad. He said he was doing farm work, practicing basketball. "I haven't gotten used to so many of my friends being gone," he said. "It isn't the same without you here, Joe. It won't be until you come back." When would that be?

Ray added one more line to his note: "All for one."

I folded up the letter. A drop of sweat dripped from my forehead to the envelope. My clothes stuck to me. Dust danced in the air. My mouth felt gritty. But getting a drink meant getting up, going out in the sun, walking to the bathroom. I stayed where I was.

Dad's letter had been written on June 14th, weeks earlier, and we were just getting it. Once the blacked-out lines were subtracted, there wasn't much left. He was being treated well, he said. He missed us very much, but he knew we would do fine without him. "How are your journals progressing, Michael and Joseph?" he asked. "You must have many observations, many thoughts to record. I look forward to reading them when I join you." He didn't say when that would be.

He ended his letter with the news that had kept Mom hovering in the heat of our room. The outcome of his hearing wasn't good, he guessed. He was being moved from Fort Missoula, but not released. The government was sending him to another camp, this time in New Mexico.

I looked at the date on the letter again. Was he already in New Mexico? What was it like there? Better? Worse? When would they stop treating him like a criminal?

Mom must have seen something on my face. Suddenly I felt her hand on my shoulder. I couldn't look at her. I couldn't speak. Her fingers tightened. I held the paper up to the sunlight, trying to see through the slashes of ink, to imagine what he was telling us that someone didn't want us to know.

"He'll be okay," Mom said, trying to smile. But her eyes gave her away. They were dark with sadness, and wet. They stayed on me as I stood.

I found pins in her sewing box. She watched me pin Dad's letter to the wall, then gave me a long hug and left. I stayed.

I got my journal from my duffel and sat on my bunk. On one page I wrote a letter to Ray. It was hard to tell him much without seeming like a complainer. I wrote about the heat, about missing the cool days at home and basketball on the dirt court at his house. I told him about finding Mae. I ended the letter with a short sentence: "One for all."

I tore out the page and used another blank page to write to Dad. I told him I had been using my journal. I didn't say anything about Mike's. I wrote some of the same things I'd written to Ray—the train trip, the size of the camp, Sandy, finding Mae. I told him what the soldier had said—that we were here for our safety. I told him I was sorry they were moving him to another place, but maybe it would be a step toward being with us again. I tried to believe those words.

Cooked through and through, I finally got up and dragged myself outside, into the shade. By the time I cooled down, I had come up with some words to keep in my journal.

> Summer heat, summer
> Dreams, trapped between thin wood walls.
> Liberties wither.

ELEVEN

We settled into a routine. The days passed, slowly at first and then in a blur of sameness. Letters came from New Mexico, from Dad. He didn't say much, but what he didn't say told us a lot. My imagination filled in the unsaid, the cut out, the inked over. My imagination gave me words and images and restless nights.

August swept by, September arrived. School started. As far as I knew, our teacher, Mr. Moffitt, didn't rise up out of the cemetery every morning. He didn't come to school wrapped in strips of cloth. He was livelier and less scary than a mummy. But he did his job blank-eyed, handing out assignments without a smile. At the end of the first week, he still hadn't called anyone by name.

"You," he said one day, looking in my direction. "Give me the subject and predicate of the sentence I've written on the board."

"Me?" I said.

"Yes," he said. "You. The one with the window-shade eyes." Then he smiled for the first time. His teeth were yellow from the cigarettes he chain-smoked. "Forgive me," he said. "You all have window-shade eyes, don't you."

I knew his subject and predicate, but I couldn't answer. The room went silent. I sat, a mummy, longing to be back in Mrs. Lynden's classroom. "I don't know," I said finally.

I decided Mr. Moffitt had probably learned how to be a teacher from one of those matchbook-cover colleges. I wasn't sure where he'd learned to be a person. I didn't look forward to seeing him every day. But school—doing the work—was okay. At home we'd had chores and jobs. At Tule Lake there were no jobs for us, and at first that seemed like a gift. But it got boring in a hurry. The adults at least had a chance to work, either in the camp or on the farms. Mom took a job as a cook in one of the mess halls.

Mike's second week at the high school, he brought home a piece of paper he'd decorated with rows of letters and numbers inside little circles. I asked him what it was.

"Mrs. Watanabe had us draw these," he said. "So we can practice typing."

"On a piece of paper?"

"There aren't any typewriters," he said. "And she can't afford to buy even one. They barely pay the Japanese American teachers."

Mom examined Mike's drawing. She lay it down and let her fingers play over the pretend keys. "Quiet, at least," she said.

"Shameful," Grandmother said.

"Tomorrow we learn how to write with imaginary chalk," Mike said.

The harvest had been coming in since we'd arrived, and now it was at its height, yet we kids weren't allowed to work the fields, even to pick our own food. But one day after school, Sandy came to our barracks driving one of the old farm trucks.

"You and Mike want to go out to the farms, Mr. Twain?" he said.

I couldn't believe it. I said yes, Mike said yes, Mom gave her approval. Grandmother looked worried but nodded. I asked Sandy if Mae could go.

"Sure," he said. "If she's willing to put up with us."

Mae was willing. Her parents agreed.

We climbed into the cab—Mae first, then me, then Mike. Plenty of room, even with Sandy behind the wheel. He smiled at us, threw the truck into gear, and eased it away, maneuvering past Phillip and another kid playing catch with a ragged old baseball. I raised my head high so they couldn't miss seeing me. The air coming in the open windows felt like heaven. I wanted to stick my head out Mike's window like a dog and let my tongue hang.

But now came the part we hadn't talked about: leaving the camp. Would they let Sandy just take us out? A trickle of sweat inched down my spine. I looked at Mike. His eyes were trained on the windshield and what lay ahead. Mae leaned back, making herself smaller between Sandy and me. She found my hand and held on tight. Her hand was smooth and soft, but strong.

"What do we do?" I said.

"Relax," Sandy said. "And smile."

Sandy waved to the gate guard. My stomach got a high-up, twisted-up feeling. I had always stayed away from the fences; there were reports of people getting too close and being shot. I hadn't been close to the gate since we'd arrived. Now I had a chance to ride right through it like a free person. I tried to smile.

The gate opened, we crept forward, and then we were past it, accelerating. Sandy shifted gears. The truck creaked and rattled. Fresh air blasted in on us. I looked back through a curtain of dust at the camp, disappearing behind us, and I imagined leaving it for good.

Mae hadn't let go of my hand. She had her head back, her hair was flying like black whips, she had a huge smile on her face and tears in her eyes. Were they from the wind, or something else? The something else was putting a lump in my throat.

Mike's head wasn't quite out the window, but it was tilted in that direction. His thick hair was standing up, his eyes were closed, and he had a look on his face that said he was somewhere else just then. He wasn't in an old truck rolling down a rough road in the middle of nowhere, in the middle of a nightmare.

He opened his eyes and stuck his head all the way outside. Twisting around, he shouted toward the camp: "We're not coming back!"

He leaned back in, laughing. We all laughed. But not for long. We already knew how our adventure would really end.

The farms were big, there were more fields than I had imagined, more people working them, more soldiers on guard. And fences and sentry towers, even out here. But I envied the workers. They got to come out here every day, breathe the air, work the earth. I would have traded them in a minute for my hours of wasting time.

Sandy drove us from farm to farm, slowing the truck whenever one of us showed an interest in something. Which was often. We were on the way back when he stopped next to a wide field of knee-high plants. I half-expected Mr. Spooner to slide down off his tractor and walk over to visit with us for a while. I could see his smile, his cowboy hat pushed back above his sweaty forehead.

"Young citizens coming out!" Sandy called to a guard. The guard nodded and raised his rifle in a kind of salute, then turned his attention to a group of workers who were digging out the bushy plants and putting something into sacks. Mike jumped down, and I followed with Mae right behind me.

We walked down a row. Heat rose from the dark ground. I smelled home. I squatted and trailed my fingers through the leaves. "What are they?" I said.

Mike picked up a four-tined digging fork and handed it to me. "See for yourself."

I set it next to the plant. The prongs settled into the soft soil. I positioned my foot and jumped on, driving the fork deep. I lifted. Dirt-covered lumps the size of my fist and bigger popped out of the ground. Potatoes. Mae picked one up. I rubbed one in my hands and watched it shed its grit. I tossed it to Mike. "Dinner," I said.

Mae made a face. "Not raw."

"Take some back," Sandy said. "Maybe your moms can do something with them."

Maybe. Mae's mom worked at the same mess hall as mine. "Can we?" I said.

"No one's going to care if you take a few," Sandy said.

We found a burlap sack and loaded a dozen potatoes into it. We sat in silence for much of the trip back. I looked at my fingernails, admiring the dirt, as we rolled through the gate.

That night after supper Mom brought us baked potatoes, still warm from the oven. We sat on the floor and cut them into steaming chunks and ate them like candy.

I got most of my war news from Mom or Mike or Grandmother, who spent time reading newspapers: the *Newell Star,* our camp paper, or the *San Francisco Chronicle.* Or magazines like *Life.* Or letters from outsiders. I also listened to rumors. Who was winning? Where? What was true? What wasn't?

Ray wrote me and sent a crisp dollar bill—an early birthday present. He asked how I was doing and said he was working long hours for a farmer who had no help. Then he gave me some other news. "Remember Mueller? His older brother Stephen is dead. His ship was sunk by a U-boat in the Atlantic somewhere. He wasn't even nineteen yet. Mueller is a moron but I feel sorry for him."

So did I. I imagined what it would be like to lose a brother, to have him ambushed at sea. I thought of how scary it would be to find yourself trapped in a sinking ship or floating alone in the dark with mountains of frigid water everywhere around you. I was thankful I was on dry land. I was thankful for the heat.

I wrote to Ray. When Mike came back to the room, I told him about Mueller's brother.

"Too bad," he said. "And he was worried about the Japs. Now he can hate the Germans too. He can look in the mirror every day and hate himself."

"You don't feel sorry for him?"

"Sure. But at least his brother had a chance to serve. And when Mueller's time comes, he can make the Nazis pay."

I wrote to Dad. I didn't tell him about Stephen Mueller. I said we were doing fine, that I was writing in my journal when I had things to say. I wondered if anyone would read my letter before Dad got it. What would they think of my keeping a journal? Spy stuff? Would they put black lines through my words?

Mike's birthday and mine were five years and two days apart. The two days arrived at the end of September. Mike's birthday was the 27th, mine was the 29th.

On the 28th, Mae's family—her parents and two older brothers—and James Ito's family—his parents and his younger sister—joined us in our room for a small celebration. Phillip showed up and I invited him in too. He didn't know we were having a party but he brought his usual gift—his smile. The evening air had cooled, but we didn't light a fire in our stove. The bodies, packed together, made their own warmth.

Mike and I opened letters from Dad wishing us happy birthday. We ate cake Mom had gotten from the mess hall. Everyone sang to us, then she gave Mike and me gifts she'd bought at the camp canteen—candy, playing cards, comic books—and big packages wrapped in brown paper. Coats. Mrs. O'Brien had sent them. I tried mine on. It was too big, but I didn't complain. At least it would keep me warm through the winter. Mike's fit him perfectly.

Mae gave me a small silver cross on a chain. Maybe she thought I needed it. But it felt good around my neck and I thanked her. Grandmother gave each of us a handkerchief. Mine was embroidered with evergreen trees and a mountain that looked like Mount Rainier. Mike's had trees and a winding blue river.

I held mine up to the wall. A few pins and we'd have a reminder of home. But she shook her head and pointed to her nose. "They are for you to use," she said. "Soon it will be time for colds."

Mom handed us two other packages wrapped in brown paper. Smaller. "Happy Birthday" written on each. My name on one, Mike's on the other.

"These were here when we returned tonight," Mom said.

Mike didn't hesitate. He tore away the paper. Inside was a book, Jules Verne's *Twenty Thousand Leagues Under the Sea*. I thought of Stephen Mueller. There was no note. "Go ahead, little brother," Mike said.

I ripped open the package. Another book. No note. But now I thought I knew who had given them to us. My book was *Tom Sawyer*, by Mark Twain. Grandmother raised her eyebrows.

The next day was my real birthday and I knew what I wanted but I knew I wouldn't get it. We still had no idea when Dad would return.

One afternoon in early October, I decided it was time to try my marbles again. We'd finally had enough rain to hold down the dust and pack the ground.

"Have you ever played?" I asked Mae.

"My brothers are experts," she said. "They taught me."

Teaching and learning are two different things, Dad sometimes said, but Mae's words sounded like a challenge. She borrowed some of her brothers' marbles, I got most of mine. The ones from Ray I left in my duffel, except for the red cat's-eye—the shooter.

We found an area of smooth dirt in the firebreak next to her barracks. She used a stick to draw a big circle and we each put ten marbles in the center. We decided to play for fun, since she didn't have any she could lose and I didn't have any I wanted to lose. The first person to capture ten would win.

After the first shot I knew she could play. She used this big smoky gray agate for a shooter. It had eyes. By the time I was up to five marbles, she crashed it into her tenth. We played again, Mae trying to hide her smile, me thinking she was good but also lucky. I did better, but she won that game and another.

"One more?" she said.

My thumb was tender, my pride dented, but I wasn't ready to quit. "Sure," I said, reaching in my pocket for the cat's-eye.

"Have you been saving that one?"

"Ray gave it to me. It's guaranteed."

She laughed. "We'll see."

I got off to a good start. Ray's marble gave me confidence. But Mae came back and won, 10–9. We called it quits.

In our first game the next day, I jumped off to a lead and held it. She took the following two, but they were close. It was fun, easy to talk, easy to smile.

When we were about to leave, Mae noticed the tip of something sticking out of the circle. She scraped around it with her stick and pulled it out. It was a seashell. But what was it doing here, hundreds of miles from the sea?

I got another stick and dug with her. I found another shell. We found more. Just below the surface. Deeper. Different sizes, different shapes. All bone-white. Old. But how old?

I imagined an ancient ocean, deeper than all the barracks at Tule Lake stood end to end. I imagined kneeling on that ocean floor where we knelt now, looking up through a forest of green seaweed at the dim blue light far overhead. I imagined Mae and me plucking living shells from the sand and pushing off and rising gracefully, backs arched, faces upturned, hair flowing, like those divers I'd once envisioned. I imagined bursting through the surface and breathing ocean air and looking around and seeing nothing but Mae and a small boat filled with pearls, my dad at the oars.

"There was an ocean here," Mae said.

"I know." I told her what I'd pictured.

She smiled and looked up at the blue sky, as if she were kneeling on the bottom of an ocean. "Where did it go?"

It wasn't a question that needed an answer, but I shrugged. I didn't know. I longed for the feel of that ocean on my skin.

That night I showed some of the shells to Mom and Grandmother. They had heard of a prehistoric ocean here.

"We can make something of these," Grandmother said.

"Something for this room," Mom said. She looked at the bare walls. I saw life in her eyes. I promised to bring them more.

Mike wasn't as impressed. He'd learned that afternoon that he and James had been accepted to work on the farm crew. After school and on weekends he would be gone, tasting freedom.

"How old do you have to be?" I asked him.

"High school."

High school. Years away. Everything was so far away.

I went out in the fading light, in the chill, and wrote about Mike getting outside the fences, about me staying in. I wrote about games of marbles. I didn't say who won. Mae wasn't there to remind me.

The next morning I saw Sandy at the mess hall. I told him about the shells. After school he brought me an army shovel, the short-handled kind with a folding blade.

"Two good things about this place," he said. "No foxholes or latrines to dig."

I'd read about foxholes, how they sometimes became soldiers' graves. I knew the word *latrines*—bad, but not much worse than the smelly outhouses we'd had at Pinedale. At least we had real bathrooms now.

Mae and I went out and dug. We unearthed shell after shell,

filling two paper bags. It felt good to work my muscles, to get my hands dirty. We took one bag to her mom, one to mine.

Our room seemed empty without Mike, but I decided I wouldn't just wait around for him. Mae and I took our marbles out to the firebreak. This time I drew the circle, for luck. Phillip and some other kids came over and watched. I was ahead 7–4 when I took aim at her big aggie, which she'd decided to put in the middle. I shot as hard and straight as I could and hit it square.

My moment of triumph was sweet. But short. Then bitter. My prized marble, my red cat's-eye, split in half. It lay in the dirt like two pieces of Humpty Dumpty.

The tearing away, Grandmother had called our leaving home. I had that feeling all over again. Smaller, but the same.

"Sorry, Joe," Mae said.

I shrugged. I kept my face down and reached out and collected both halves, then the aggie. But it was the last shot I made. I couldn't get any of my other marbles working; my eyes weren't quite right.

We went back to my room. Mom and Grandmother and Mae's mom were working, sitting on sturdy, bare-wood benches at a small, square-topped table. Mom had bribed two of the camp carpenters with extra desserts and they'd made us furniture out of scraps of wood.

Once, Mom would have stood in Dad's shadow and waited for him to figure out a way to take care of our family's needs. He would have waded into the give-and-take with whoever could help us. But he wasn't here now. She was. I felt proud of her for taking over and sorry that she had to. And sorrier still for the reason why.

I could barely believe what Grandmother and our mothers had done. They'd glued the shells together to make flowers, and they were painting them with red fingernail polish. They looked real, even up close. Mae and I stood over the women and watched. From time to time Grandmother would look up at me and smile.

When we returned from supper, I sat by the stove with my journal and stared at the flowers in their jars, where they were drying. I imagined they were real, that I could smell them. It was the Mrs. Lynden smell.

I wrote about Mae and me, digging through old ocean bottom, uncovering ancient skeletons. I wrote about our mothers turning them into wondrous new flowers.

> *Blossoms from ageless*
> *Seabeds, from nimble fingers.*
> *Memories from home.*

As October wore on, more flowers bloomed in our room, in Mae's. She and I would collect the shells; our moms and my grandmother would transform them. They kept some, gave some away, sold some to people who insisted on paying. Our moms rewarded us with coupons to take to the canteen, as long as we would go by the post office to mail letters. It was a long walk—a mile one way—but worth it, even as the wind blew colder and the days grew darker. At the canteen there was candy and soda pop and a feeling, for a little while, that life was normal.

I heard of a place at camp where basketball was being played. I searched it out on a Saturday morning, when I thought the chances of finding a game were good. I found a crowd of older boys and young men, waiting on the sidelines of a rough dirt court with baskets and backboards mounted on poles at each end. On the court, two teams were going at each other, hard. Quick dribbles and clean passes and pretty shots were nowhere in sight. Instead there were fouls and flying bodies and curses.

The game ended. Five more young men took the court to replace the losing team. I crowded my way to the sideline and toed the dirt. It was wet and heavy. It reminded me of our muddy court at Ray's house.

Another game started. More pushing and banging. Shots clanged off the rims. Some of the players looked as if they'd never touched a basketball before, but they were good with the rugged stuff.

"How do you get in this game?" I asked a guy standing next to me.

He looked down at me. I waited for an answer. His attention went back to the game, as if he hadn't heard me.

"How do you?" I said.

This time he didn't even spare a glance.

"Don't waste your time, shorty," a guy on the other side of me said.

I looked up, to make sure he was talking to me. "Joe."

"Big boys' game, Joe," he said. "Spend all day here, you won't get in. You need a team." He sized me up and down. "You need about six years and twelve inches."

"I'm better than these guys," I said. "I could go through them like a slick fish. I could sink baskets like a machine."

"Doesn't matter. You won't get out there. If you did, you'd get trampled. They'd carry you off on a board."

I'd run out of things to say. I decided he was right, but I stayed for a while anyway, showing him I wasn't taking him at his word.

He got into the next game of animal ball; so did the guy who hadn't talked to me. They were both unskilled, but tried to make up for it with football tactics. I imagined myself stealing the ball from them, racing downcourt to score. I imagined the crowd of bystanders cheering.

The cold was seeping into my bones. I left, certain that nobody even noticed. On my slow walk back to our barracks, I thought about returning sometime, but what good would it do?

Maybe in four years. Maybe when I was eight inches taller and too fast to get roughed up. But by then I'd be long gone. I prayed I'd be long gone.

The end of October approached. At home this would have meant preparing for Halloween. At Tule Lake it meant more of the same. More days of wasting time and strange meals like rice balls and bologna. And talk of the war.

At school, Mr. Moffitt acted as if the war were off-limits. He almost never mentioned it, and when he did it was in a hushed, wheezy voice with cautious, sideways glances. Maybe he thought we would pass his useless information along to Japanese spies, or gloat if he mentioned a Japanese victory somewhere. Maybe he didn't realize we were young citizens.

The war news I got at school came before or after class or at lunch or recess. It came from kids whose teachers did talk about the war.

"Miss Armstrong says we're holding our own in the Pacific," Phillip told me and Mae on the way home from school one day. His smile glowed in the afternoon gloom.

"What's that mean?" I said.

"She read us an article from a Washington, D.C., newspaper. It said that since the battle of Midway, we've been slowing the Japanese progress. We've made some of our own. We've sunk their ships and beaten back their armies."

"Maybe the war will end soon," Mae said. "The dying will end. We could leave here."

I had heard of the battle of Midway while we were at Pinedale. It was a big and important battle and our navy had crippled the Japanese navy. "They shouldn't have bullied us," I said.

The next morning Phillip joined us for the walk to school. His smile was gone. He didn't talk as we trudged along.

"What's the matter?" Mae asked.

He didn't answer for a minute. Then: "This morning I told my dad what Miss Armstrong said. He told me I was being fed American lies."

"*You're* an American," I said.

Phillip shook his head, as if he didn't want to hear me. "'Only a fool would believe them,' my dad said. 'The Japanese will not give up. They will never surrender. The Americans have never fought anyone like the Japanese.'"

I lay in my bunk that night and listened to Mike and Mom and Grandmother speak in hushed voices of faraway battles and losses and gains and what it all meant. They no longer minded if I heard—if I joined in, even—but what could I add? Lies? How would I know? The outside world might as well have been off in the stars.

What was happening to the people back home? Had the older brothers all gone off to fight? Was Stephen Mueller just the first to die? Were the women all working in factories? Fifteen thousand Americans were locked behind Tule Lake's fences. How could we have helped?

Mae and Phillip and I were outside with some other kids the afternoon of October 31st when Sandy and Mike drove up in a farm truck. They unloaded big muddy knobs from the back while we gathered around.

"Turnips," Mike said, and at first I thought he was joking. They were more the size of melons. Or pumpkins.

"For jack-o'-lanterns," Sandy announced, holding up an extra-big one, brushing off some mud. "Not quite as easy to carve, but they'll do." He handed out pocketknives to the kids as they came forward to choose. Mae and Phillip and I waited for some of the younger ones to get a chance, but when we finally stepped up, Sandy gave us the one he was holding. He gave us his own knife. "Maybe you three can work together on this one," he said. "Make your mothers proud."

"Carve the face of your favorite Nazi," Mike said to the kids.

I pictured Hitler, not sure how we could make that mustache of his, the soup-bowl haircut. "Let's make a scary one," I said to Mae and Phillip. "Something to keep the Nazis away." And the war. And maybe scare the government into freeing my dad.

We sat in the dirt with the rest of the kids and took turns hollowing and carving. When we were done, our jack-o'-lantern didn't look exactly like a jack-o'-lantern. Or Hitler. But it was good. It had a hollowed-out head with a removable lid, straight-down bangs, whisker lines carved below its piggish nose, wide, crazy eyes, and a snarl of a mouth filled with crooked teeth.

Mom and Grandmother and Mae's parents came out and

admired its ugly scowl. They gave us coupons for the canteen, where we bought candles and candy corn. Phillip's parents kept their sour faces in their room. After dark he goose-stepped around us wearing a Nazi helmet carved from a turnip. We ate candy and put the jack-o'-lanterns in a half-circle and lit the candles in them. Their faces flickered in the cold wind, raising goose bumps on my arms. For the first time in a long time, I prayed.

The next day a letter came from Dad. If he had written us any real news, it had been sliced away or blacked out. "I love all of you," he said at the bottom. "I wish I could be there to help. Thank you for being strong."

Mike held the letter up to the window, to the evening's fading light. He peered at the paper. "Dad says the food's improving," Mike said. "Lobster, french fries, pheasant under glass, home-made rolls, angel food cake with strawberries and whipped cream, chocolate malts with every meal. The waiters all wear tuxedos and call him 'sir.'"

Mom and Grandmother, sitting at our table, giggled.

I shouldered in next to Mike and studied the letter. "Dad also says he had a judo match last night," I said, squinting at the blacked-over words. "He whipped the camp commander, Colonel"—I glanced outside, at an army car easing past our barracks—"Dodge. So now Dad's in charge of the whole place. He's letting everyone go home, then he and Joe Louis and King Kong are coming up here to challenge the Tule Lake bosses. Dad's already made our reservations for the train ride home to Thomas."

For a quick moment I pretended it was all true. But Mom and

Grandmother laughed and brought me back to reality. I looked again at the last words of Dad's letter—his real words, thanking us for being strong.

I didn't feel strong. I wanted him with us. I wondered what he was saying to the government people. Why wouldn't they let him go?

I pinned his letter to the wall, next to the other ones, next to the pictures.

After that I would often stop and read them, imagining him saying the words, saying the made-up words. Sometimes his voice wouldn't come right away and I would get scared. I would read the sentences over and over until I could hear it.

TWELVE

Except for the increasing cold, except for seeing Phillip less and less, the days seemed the same, like the Canada geese that swarmed over the flat country around us on their way to somewhere far-off and warm. One would spread its wings and leave, but another just like it would take its place. All the days we spent huddled around our little stove seemed like one day. All the hours at school, one long hour, the countless games of marbles, one game. The walks with Mike or Mae, talks of the war, our futures, the endless days of waiting. All the same. All one. When would they end? When would I see Dad?

Christmas Eve arrived, a shadow of the ones I remembered. We went to a party at the mess hall for people in our block. Little kids sang "Silent Night" off-key and decorated a sparse-limbed tree with scraps of cloth and paper. The refreshments were too familiar. Graham crackers and peanut butter. Canned fruit.

I saw forced smiles and cheer and people dressed up in whatever decent clothes they had, pretending not to notice if someone else's were patched or threadbare or faded. I hoped no one would look closely at mine. I wore a white shirt, frayed at the cuffs, my church slacks, hovering over my ankles, and my only pair of shoes, scuffed and gnawing at my toes. Both Mom and Mike had offered to buy me something new at the dry goods canteen or through the Montgomery Ward catalog, but I told them no. They were going without new clothes and not complaining. I could, too.

Mae was there with her family. She brought me warm punch. Her hair was combed neatly, her blue dress looked almost new but shorter than when I had seen her wear it at St. Paul's. "You look very dressy tonight, Joseph."

"Church clothes."

She raised an eyebrow and I waited for her to say something about me attending services again. But she didn't.

"You look nice, too," I said, remembering my manners.

"Church clothes," she said. "But you don't have to dress up to go to church here." She smiled.

"Huh," I said.

Phillip wasn't at the party. I didn't know if his family was Buddhist or if it was just that his father was a humbug about Christmas the way he seemed to be about other things.

The next morning we opened gifts from the canteen—magazines, combs, candy—or from old neighbors. Ray sent me a new baseball. I had sent him nothing but a wish for a merry Christmas on a card I made myself.

I put his gift in my duffel. I didn't plan to take it outside. An earlier snow had melted and turned the thawing dirt into a sea of mud that reached in every direction outside our barracks. I would save the baseball for spring. Or home. I wondered if Ray's basketball court had gone soft with rain.

The old year—1942—ended. I was glad to see it go. The new one didn't seem much different. At first. But January soon brought excitement, rolling across Tule Lake like a tsunami.

Mike burst into the room one afternoon, nearly ripping through the line full of drying clothes Mom had strung from wall to wall. He barely noticed. His smile was wide. Dad-is-being-freed wide. The-war-is-over wide. "They're going to let us fight!"

"Who?" Mom said.

"Us." He paced back and forth. "Nisei. They told us at school. The army's going to recruit an all-Nisei combat team."

"How many men?" Mom said. She wasn't smiling. Grandmother wasn't smiling. I had to force myself.

"Five thousand to start with. Maybe more later."

"They will be drafted?" Mom said.

"Volunteers."

"Good," Grandmother said. She and Mom went back to their flower making, done talking about it. At seventeen, Mike was barely old enough to join the army, and then only with a parent's permission. I could see on Mom's face that there would be no permission.

Mike looked at me, but I didn't know what to say. His exciting news didn't excite me. "Huh," I said.

He turned around and left.

Opinions blossomed like flowers, or weeds. The *Newell Star* ran articles and editorials and letters. I heard adults talking, discussing, arguing, at the mess hall, the canteen, standing in buzzing clusters in the cold. Kids brought their parents' ideas to school with them and debated them in the classroom. Not in my classroom, though, where Mr. Moffitt started and ended the discussion with a sneer and a short, ugly comment. "Jap boys fighting for us?" he said. "Ridiculous."

I had my opinion, but my opinion changed as often as Mr. Moffitt slid another Chesterfield between his mustard-colored fingers and lit it. Now we'll get to prove ourselves, I'd think one minute. Now we'll be treated like Americans. This is an opportunity. In the next instant I'd think of Mike, that he'd be eighteen in less than a year. And the opportunity put on a scary mask that made me want to hide.

When I joined the school conversations—when I wasn't under Mr. Moffitt's buzzard-eyed watch—I didn't know which opinion to give. And Dad had once told me that it's hard to learn anything when all you can hear is yourself. So I mostly listened.

A lot of the kids said their families were happy about the volunteer unit. But some weren't. Phillip's, for instance. "My dad says it's a slap in the face," he said one morning before school. "Our rights have been taken away along with our homes and most of what we owned, and now we're being asked to give our young men too." It sounded like a little speech, as if he'd memorized his dad's words.

"What does Miss Armstrong say?" I asked. Phillip was practically in love with Miss Armstrong.

"I don't listen to her anymore," Phillip said.

"You should," Mae said. "'Pride goeth before destruction, and a haughty spirit before a fall.'"

"What's that mean?" Phillip said.

"It's from the Bible," I said.

"I don't know the Bible," Phillip said.

"It means people who think they know it all are asking for trouble," Mae said.

"To lose is to win," I said. "You're supposed to be humble."

"My dad's tired of being humble," Phillip said. He wasn't smiling.

Sometimes there were differences of opinion within a family. Ours was one of those. Mike hated what had been done to us, but he also hated not being able to fight, to prove he was a loyal American. Now he had a chance to show that the government had been wrong, to prove that his people didn't deserve to be locked up behind barbed wire.

Grandmother sat on the opposite side of the argument. "Government," she said a few days after the announcement. "They treat our children like dogs yet want them to fight like men." She sounded like Phillip's dad. She was looking at Mike when she said it. But he lay on his bunk, his hands behind his head, staring at the ceiling. A smile was frozen on his face. I wondered if he'd even heard her.

"Just show me where to sign up," he said. "I can't wait."

"You're too young," Mom said.

"If you give your permission…?" he said.

"I won't give permission," Mom said, and Grandmother nodded.

"Ask Dad," Mike said.

"Your father isn't here. And I know his answer."

"I'll be eighteen in eight months," Mike said. "Then I'll need no permission."

Mom walked to the window. Her back was to us as she looked out at the mud and homely buildings and cold, gray sky. "You will still be part of this family," she said. "But when you are eighteen you can make your own mistakes." I figured Mike's smile would fade. It didn't. He was expecting her words, willing to be patient. Part of me wanted to speak up for him; part of me was relieved that Mom had told him no, that Grandmother was in Mom's corner.

I did some figuring. By the time Mike turned eighteen and joined the army and got trained, it could be the end of 1943, maybe even 1944. The war could be over. I had heard of more victories by the navy in the Pacific, that the tide might be turning. But what about Europe? Who was winning that war? Would he be sent there to fight Hitler's army? I wanted Dad with us. I wanted him to talk to Mike.

By late January, discussions over the combat team had faded a little. Then Mom came home from work one night with more news. "They want us to register," she announced.

"Register?" Grandmother said.

"For what?" Mike said.

Mom shrugged. "They say it's because of our boys going in the army. And young people going off to college. The government wants to see who is eligible."

"How will registering tell them that?" Mike said.

"We're already registered," I said.

"They know our names and who we are," Grandmother said. "They have given us numbers. We are here, under guard. What more do they want?"

"Loyalty," Mom said. "We have to complete a form to prove our loyalty."

Mr. Moffitt thought registration was a good idea. "The Japanese should be happy to do their duty," he said at school the next day. He liked to talk about us as if we weren't there. "They should welcome the opportunity to distinguish themselves from the riffraff." His words sounded familiar. I remembered the newspaper article that said we should cheerfully accept relocation.

Most kids didn't know much about what was happening, but they were willing to start rumors or keep them going.

"My dad says this might be a way for us to get out of this place earlier," Mae said on the way home for lunch. "If we say the right things, maybe they'll trust us."

"But where will they send us?" Phillip said. "My dad says they'll use this registration as an excuse to ship us to Japan. He says he will sign nothing."

"Rumors have spread like plague," Mom said when we were in our room that night. "But I have learned some things."

"As have I," Grandmother said.

"Me, too," Mike said.

They all looked at me. "I heard a rumor," I said. "Anyone who fills out the registration form left-handed will be sent to Japan on the next ship."

Mike was left-handed. He tried to frown at me. He smiled instead. Mom and Grandmother shook their heads.

"Let's sit and talk," Mom said, and we did.

"The form is a questionnaire," Mom said.

"Many questions," Grandmother said.

"Sixty," Mom said. "Some confusing ones."

"I have to fill one out," Mike said. "Everyone seventeen and older, they told us at school."

Seventeen. Not me. I was glad. Sixty questions was way too many. But I didn't like the idea of Mike registering. It meant he was that much closer to joining the army.

We talked, huddled around our little stove, until it was time for supper, then walked through the cold and over frozen ground to the mess hall. It was noisier than usual. People were standing in groups, visiting from table to table. Mae and her family came in and sat at our table with us, as they often did. It was good sitting close, having friends to talk to while we ate. A month earlier, we had complained of being bored. Now that wasn't a problem.

Talk continued over the next days. Fact. Rumor. I tried to spread the left-handed one at school, but no one took it seriously enough to pass it on.

On February 10th there was a big meeting in the mess hall for everyone in our block—about three hundred people. Registration was supposed to begin, but there were so many questions about the questions that most people refused to fill out the form until they got answers. And until they found out for sure what was behind the questionnaire. People had their own ideas about what questions the government wanted answered. Who are the good guys? Who are the bad guys? Who should go into the army? Who should be sent to Japan? Who can go off to school? Who can be released from the camps? This thought—that we might be allowed to return home, or at least live outside the fences—stirred excitement into the bad feelings about registration.

I asked Sandy if he knew anything. All he could give me was a sad face. "I'm just a soldier, Joe," he said. "I hear the same rumors you do. I just hope the good ones are true."

"We have to go back tonight," Mom announced about a week later. "The block manager came around. He said come prepared to complete the questionnaires."

Grandmother sat. "Will you help me with mine, Joseph?"

She could read as well as I could, maybe better, but sometimes the meanings of words escaped her. She fidgeted nervously with the hem of her dress. "Sure," I said. "Together we'll really foul it up."

The mess hall was crowded. It smelled of that night's supper: mutton and fried potatoes and canned peas. Questions filled the stale air. The men who had represented us at meetings with the government got up and gave us empty answers. A few people— probably their families—clapped when they were finished.

"Stooges," Mike said.

The government guy gave us more answers. His main answer was a threat. Anyone who refused to register could be prose- cuted under something called the Espionage Act. "The penalty," he said, "is ten thousand dollars or twenty years in prison or both."

He got no applause. The crowd reacted with groans and angry muttering and a few chuckles. If everyone in the mess hall pooled their money it wouldn't amount to ten thousand dollars.

"We are already in prison," Grandmother said.

Phillip's dad stood. "What about numbers twenty-seven and twenty-eight?" he shouted.

"Answer 'em," the government man growled. "If you're smart, yes and yes."

Phillip's dad took his mom's hand and helped her up. Phillip stood. They walked from the hall.

We got in lines and brought forms back to our table. I sat with Grandmother. We puzzled over the questions while Mom and Mike worked across from us. We got to number 27: "Are you willing to serve in the armed forces of the United States on combat duty, wherever ordered?"

"They want me to answer this?" Grandmother asked me.

"All of them, Grandmother," Mike said. I looked at his form. He was nearly finished. Left-handed.

Grandmother shook her head. "Government," she said. She answered yes.

Number 28 asked if she was willing to swear allegiance to the United States and renounce any allegiance to the Japanese emperor or any other foreign government.

She studied the question.

"Do you know what it means, Grandmother?" I said.

"It's one of the trick ones I have heard about."

"It is," Mom said. She was stuck on the same question.

"Your mother and I are not citizens here," Grandmother said. "We cannot become citizens. How can I swear allegiance to a country that has no allegiance to me? How can I deny allegiance to Japan if this country won't allow me to stay here? Where would I go?"

"Dad isn't a citizen either," I said.

"How will he answer?" Grandmother asked Mom.

"I don't know," Mom said. "I wrote to him and asked but he hasn't written back."

"Yes-yes," Mike said. "Dad's an American."

"After all he has been through?" Grandmother said.

"Yes-yes," Mike said. "Same as me."

Me, too. I didn't have to answer the questionnaire. But I knew how I would have answered if I'd been old enough. With Mike. Yes and yes and where do I sign up? If Mike's going to war, so am I.

Mom and Grandmother skipped number 28. I helped Grandmother through the rest of the questions. Mike finished. Mom finished. Except for number 28.

"I think Michael is right," she said finally. She answered yes.

Now it was Grandmother's turn. "Trick question," she said, staring at the paper. We sat while people went to the front and handed in their forms and filed out. I wanted her to answer yes, but she'd asked for my help, not my advice. Grandmother liked to give advice, not get it.

Only a handful of people remained when she finally made her decision. "I have not felt an allegiance to the emperor since I left Japan twenty years ago," she said. "How can I renounce anything?" She drummed her fingers on the tabletop. "But I cannot be left without a country." She answered no.

We honored her choice with silence. But I worried about what the decision would mean. Would she get deported to Japan? There were already people at the camp requesting repatriation, which meant they wanted to go back, or in the case of Nisei, go for the first time. Grandmother wasn't one of those. She wanted to stay with us. But would she have a choice? We handed in the forms and left.

The next day Mae and I walked back to the barracks together after school. She was excited, talking about possibilities. Now that her parents had sworn their loyalty, there was a chance her family could leave the camp. She had heard them talking about getting a sponsor, which meant the government might allow her family to settle somewhere locally, maybe on a farm, and live like regular people.

"Maybe your family could find a sponsor close to us, Joe," she said. "We would have friends nearby." The thought raised my heartbeat like a run through knee-deep water. I imagined being outside the fences, walking with Dad, living in a house, going to a real school, lying in a grass field and looking up at the stars, never having to return to Tule.

What if we *could* get out of the camp? Mike would be happy. Maybe he wouldn't be so eager to join the army.

He was waiting outside for me when I got back to the barracks. "I don't want Grandmother to overhear," he said, walking me away from the thin wood walls of our building.

"What?" I said.

"I've heard more talk of letting Japanese Americans out of the camps."

"Me, too," I said.

"They won't let Grandmother go."

I didn't want to hear it. I didn't want to believe it. "Why?"

"She answered no. She'll be considered disloyal. They'll let her out when Japan is bombed into the ocean."

I guessed he was right. And I knew if Grandmother stayed, so would we. We wouldn't leave her. Mae's possibilities faded like my memories of home. "She said she would fight." But as soon as I said it I had to smile at the picture of Grandmother carrying a rifle across an open field with shells exploding all around her, raining chunks of dirt down on her helmet.

Mike smiled, too. "She's tough enough."

"How could an old woman be a threat to the government?" I said.

"All people who answered no will be treated the same. That's what everyone is saying. You're going to be here a while, Joe."

"But you're not."

"Eight months. Then I'll be gone."

Five minutes earlier I would have reminded him of an alternative: leaving camp, living a normal life with us. Now that wasn't a choice. Maybe it never was. The FBI considered Dad dangerous; maybe they wouldn't release any of us. "You have to?"

"The government has never seen a Hanada fight. Neither have the Nazis. I have to show them."

I went inside, puffed up by Mike's brave words, scared by them at the same time. A letter had arrived from Dad.

"I answered yes to both questions," he wrote. Mike had been right. "I want to see my family again, as soon as possible. Maybe saying yes will help." I pinned his letter to the wall next to his others, like notes from someone marooned on a desert island, retrieved by someone marooned on another.

Grandmother was working with her shells. For the first time in a long time I sat down with my journal. The days of sameness had inspired me to write nothing. Now something—many things—had happened. I just needed to find the words. I began with a haiku.

Winter sun creeps cold,
Above the horse's collar.
Fears blossom below.

THIRTEEN

Winter faded. Men transformed bare stretches of dirt into baseball fields. Games began—baseball, softball—played by boys, girls, men. Crowds of people came just to watch. I played often, Mike seldom. Sometimes the games were organized, sometimes we just showed up and chose teams. While we played it was easier to imagine we were outside the fences, away from the emptiness of Tule.

When I wasn't playing ball, I passed my time with Mike or Mae or Phillip or some of the other kids from school. Or by myself. Sometimes I would take my journal and walk, observing, thinking about what I saw, thinking about words.

Spring turned into summer. The weather became cloudless and hot. Mike graduated. To what? I tried not to think about it. The school year ended for me, too. I didn't miss Mr. Moffitt, and I didn't really miss school. It had gotten hard for me to think of one without the other.

But now there were more hours to fill. Kids in our block spent their days at the baseball fields, walking to the canteen, looking for shade, sitting, reading comic books, talking, wasting time. Mae and I still dug for shells. We still played marbles.

Some other guys and I formed a baseball team. We called it a team, anyway. When our ball fell apart, I finally brought out the one I'd gotten from Ray. Soon it was scuffed and dirty. I didn't care, I told myself. There were other baseballs out there. And someday I'd be able to walk into a store and buy one.

After sundown the air cooled and we played hide-and-seek or tag. Or war. Always good guys and Nazis.

Sometimes there would be entertainment—a talent show, a dance, a scratchy-looking movie at the mess hall or outside. But most of the time I wouldn't go. Most of the time, once Mike got home from the farm, I wanted to be with him.

We'd seen less and less of Phillip. He'd told us his parents had answered no to the two big questions on the form. Now they kept him away from most of the other kids. They made him get new friends. They kept him busy with Japanese-language classes.

Mae and I were walking to the canteen one day when he came out of a barracks, walking toward us. "How are you doing, Phillip?" I said when we got close.

Nothing. He didn't even look. We stopped. He kept going, eyes straight ahead. I watched him walk past like a mummy. "Phillip?" I said to his back. Nothing.

"Don't bother, Joe," Mae said.

"What's the matter with him?"

"I talked to him once after school got out," she said. "When no one was around. He's not going back to regular school in the fall. His parents have forbidden him to speak English."

"You're kidding."

"No. There are many others too."

We continued on toward the canteen while I tried to get used to the idea of never talking to Phillip again. I couldn't.

Summer wore on. On July 4th there was a carnival with food and games. It was fun, a change from the day-to-day, a chance to honor our country's birthday. But many people stayed away.

A few weeks later I woke to hammering, the sounds of machinery. Mom and I went outside and followed the noises. They led us toward the fences.

The scenery was changing. Crews of men were busy, building new fences. One was tall, Cyclone and barbed wire. Familiar. But thirty or forty feet beyond it a shorter wood-and-barbed-wire barrier was going up. Other crews were hammering and sawing, putting together some kind of wood framework next to the Cyclone fence.

"I have heard talk of this," Mom said.

"What's happening?" I asked her.

"Two fences now," Mom said. "No-man's-land in between. More guard towers."

"Why?" I said. "No one's gotten out. Has anyone ever tried?"

"They are afraid someone will."

"Who?"

"No-Nos. All the people who answered no and no from the nine other camps are being sent here. Some people here will be sent to those camps."

"No-Nos," I said. Who had given them that name?

The fences continued to go up as summer wore on. Guard towers took shape. More soldiers came in to man them or walk the perimeter with their guns. Tanks rolled in and set up in the army area with their cannons facing us.

"Don't worry about it," Sandy told me one day. "This is what the army calls a show of force."

"They're not going to shoot us?"

"There are some unhappy people coming here," he said. "Some troublemakers, probably. But nobody's going to shoot anybody."

I felt better. But it was hard to ignore the extra soldiers, the tanks, the reason for their coming. I wasn't looking forward to the arrival of the No-Nos.

The harvest began, and Mike came back from the fields tired and dirty but with life in his eyes. He saw better things to come, I knew: freedom and adventure, a chance to prove himself. Like Tom Sawyer making plans for a trip downriver, picturing himself on his raft, full of wonder at what might lie around the bend.

August blurred by. Molly, the granddaughter of Grandmother's friend Mrs. Nomura, left camp to go off to college in Illinois. Otherwise, the month seemed much like July. But Molly's leaving meant September was next. And my birthday. And Mike's.

September arrived, unwelcome. School started. Eighth grade. Mrs. Berger was my teacher. A nice lady who learned my name the first day, who seemed glad to be teaching us. But how many years would it be before I saw a real school? The days turned darker, both outside and inside our apartment, where Mom and Grandmother grew more and more quiet. I would look up from something and see them staring at Mike as if they were drinking him in.

One warm afternoon Mae was at her embroidery class, Mike was working. I decided to take a walk with my journal. As I headed toward the gate, I noticed other people going in the same direction. Four families carrying bags and boxes and luggage. Three young men, small duffels in their hands, walking tall. Two teenage girls carrying suitcases, smiling.

I fell in close behind the young men, trying to match their long strides. We neared the gate. More people were already there, forming groups. An army sergeant, tall and wiry, shook hands with the men I had followed and others standing near us. Army recruits. I thought of Mike. I moved up close to the sergeant with a sudden wish in the front of my mind: He would take me; Mike wouldn't have to go.

The sergeant noticed me standing there. "Your little brother come along to say good-bye?" he asked the young guy closest to me. Little brother? We looked nothing alike.

"New recruit, I think, Sergeant," the guy said, smiling.

I nodded. "I'm thinking about it," I said, lowering my voice.

The sergeant grinned down at me. I waited for him to tell me to come back in six years and twelve inches. "Your momma wouldn't like that, little son," the sergeant said. "But you'll get your chance. You're the kind of soldier the army's looking for."

What kind was that? I wondered. "I'm good with Morse code," I said. "Quick and accurate."

"You keep workin' on it, lad. The Signal Corps will be after you like a trophy catfish."

"When?" I said. I had been forced to become a patient person, but my newfound patience had its limits.

"When you're ready," the sergeant said. "When your momma's ready. When we're ready. When Father Time's ready."

"Oh," I said. That was too many people to get ready. I wouldn't be taking Mike's place. I wandered away and sat on the ground close by to watch the goings-on.

A couple of months earlier, traffic in and out of the gate had been like a slow drip from a faucet. Farm workers. Guards. Government people. Delivery people. A few young men leaving for the army. A few students going off to college in the East.

Now it was all those plus more. Thousands more, I had heard. Some of these families were leaving for homes outside the camp, sometimes far away. I could see them trying not to smile too widely but not always succeeding. Others—those who didn't have to cover up smiles—were moving to other camps to make way for the new group moving in. No-Nos. They were supposed to begin arriving any day.

Now more people came. Lines formed. Cars and buses pulled up to wait. Smiling families got in cars driven by white men and women who greeted them with more smiles. Other families walked through the gate and up the road toward the highway and railroad tracks. Students got on one bus, army recruits on another. Cars left. Buses left. For a while the entrance was empty, the sentries had nothing to do.

In the distance a train whistle sounded. The train approached, chuffing, slowing, braking. I waited. The army sentries suddenly went on alert. Some went outside the gate and formed a line, rifles angled across their chests. Three jeeps full of police-capped wardens and two full of immigration guys with their flat-brimmed hats raced past me and up to the gate. They piled out, all business, guns and leather and serious faces. I felt my stomach rise. Other people stopped to look, and the wardens told them to clear a space.

Someone was coming. I thought I knew who. Bad guys. No-Nos.

The uniformed men stood tall. Some paced or shifted their weight from foot to foot. Some fingered their guns. They waited.

And then the first of the arrivals walked into view. An old man and woman, weighed down with bags. A family with three small kids. A couple with two teenage boys. None of them looked like bad guys. More came. Lots of old people wearing lost expressions. More families.

Young men arrived, walking shoulder to shoulder, swaggering, meeting the uniforms' stares. Smiling. Frowning. Blank-faced. But cocky. Bad guys, maybe.

All the No-Nos lined up at tables to fill out papers once more. A young man glanced at me, then away, the way Mr. Moffitt did—I wasn't good enough, I was some kind of traitor. The old people were dressed in layers of winter clothes. Their faces glistened in the sun. Worn down, they sat on boxes and suitcases while they waited.

Finally it was time for all of them to go, for the wardens to herd them to their barracks. One old woman got up and gestured to her husband but he shook his head and kept sitting. She looked around anxiously. She looked at me.

I got up. I went to them. "Would you like some help, Grand-mother?" I said. The old man peered up at me. His face was carved with wrinkles.

"You do lessons?" the old woman said, glancing at my journal. I slipped it inside my shirt. "I'm doing nothing."

"Please, then." She said something to the old man in Japanese. He struggled to his feet. I tied a bag over my shoulder and picked up the man's suitcase and one of the woman's. Now she had only one to carry. All he had was a small duffel.

We walked, trying to keep in sight of the main group. But we didn't have to worry. A warden was lagging behind, keeping an eye on us. Maybe he thought the old man and woman were going to make a getaway.

My back and arms grew weary, sweat trickled down my face. Their barracks was past ours, a long walk, and the old man was having a hard time putting one foot in front of the other. I stopped to shift my load once, to give them a chance to rest, and then we were off again.

Finally we arrived. A warden directed us to an apartment. A block manager checked the couple's names—Masao and Eiko Terada—off a list. I carried their belongings inside. Mr. Terada sat on a bare bunk while his wife looked around the room. It looked just like ours but emptier. She shrugged and said something to her husband.

He managed a sad-eyed smile. "*Shikata ga nai.*"

I had heard the expression before, even before we'd left the White River Valley. I knew what it meant. But Mrs. Terada translated for me. "Means, 'It cannot be helped,'" she said.

I glanced at the walls. "Government," I said.

She grinned at me. It was Grandmother's grin. "Yes." She found her purse and took out a wrinkled dollar bill and held it out to me. "For you."

I backed toward the door. "I can't take it," I said.

"You saved us," she said, still reaching out with the money.

I held up my arm and showed her my bicep. I flexed it. "I'm trying to get stronger," I said. "For sports. Thank you for letting me carry your things." I started through the door.

"What is your name?" she said.

"Joe," I called back. "Joe Hanada."

I went home and told Grandmother how nice Mrs. Terada

was. I told her she should arrange a visit. Maybe she could add Mrs. Terada to her list of friends.

But not all No-Nos were nice. Before, even though everyone in camp believed what was happening was wrong, most expressed their beliefs quietly, they went along, they hoped time would return their lives to normal. But many No-Nos arrived with different attitudes, different loyalties, and wore them like badges. And even though none were put in barracks in our block, they were free to roam the camp, harassing people who didn't share their beliefs. I thought the feeling at the camp was ugly before. Now it was worse.

Mike kept doing his job at the farms. I hoped he would like it so much he wouldn't want to leave it. But what then? The job would end after harvest, soon after his birthday. His eighteenth birthday. Then what would hold him? Winter behind barbed wire? Two hundred chilly days of wasted time? Two hundred dark nights hunched over a stove?

One night after supper he asked me if I wanted to play catch. "I'll get my ball," I said.

"I've got a special one," he said.

We went out to the firebreak. He opened up a bread bag and took out the special ball. But it wasn't a ball. It was a hockey puck–shaped chunk of the brined liver they served us too often at the mess hall. He slammed it to the hard dirt. It bounced back up.

"Perfect," I said.

We tossed it back and forth, close together at first, then moving out. When we missed, it hit the ground and caromed off in crazy directions, gathering dust, which ended up—greasy—on our hands and clothes. We laughed. People walked by, giving us looks.

"We need a bat," Mike said.

"Yeah," I said. "Maybe one of those stale loaves of bread we had for lunch today."

We played until dirt caked our hands and dusk had settled in and we were tired of laughing. Then Mike ran toward the fence and launched the lump of insides far into the air, far out over the fence. "For the coyotes," he said.

"I hope they survive," I said. We laughed.

"Dogs," someone said. I turned back toward our barracks. Twenty feet away three guys were standing, half-slouching, hands jammed in their pockets. Mike's age, probably, maybe older. No-Nos.

"What?" Mike said, stepping in front of me.

"Dogs," the tallest one repeated. "The white sentries watch you from their towers and think what playful foot-lickers you are, how you are so grateful to be here." His friends laughed, forced and loud. I looked around; no one else was nearby. My insides rumbled.

"Dogs?" Mike's shoulders squared, his hands came up, his knees flexed a fraction of an inch. I moved up next to him. My legs felt watery, suddenly. But I could help, maybe. He'd taught me a few things. Dad had taught me a few things. "Dogs are brave and quick and fight to protect their homes," Mike said. "Hyenas laugh stupidly and smell bad and follow the stink of death."

The smirks on the three guys' faces disappeared. They strutted toward us and stopped a stride away. In my throat a fat frog expanded its chin pouch until I could barely breathe. "There are three of us," the tall guy in the middle said. "One of you. So who is stupid?"

"*Two* of us," Mike said, and my throat emptied, my heart swelled.

The hyenas giggled.

"You think you have it bad here?" Mike said. "You want to go to Japan?"

The middle guy nodded.

"Then you *are* the stupid one," Mike said, and the guy frowned. The hyena on our right sidled away from the pack, working his way behind us. I half-turned to watch, but Mike seemed to ignore him. "Japan isn't your country any more than Italy or Poland or Germany is the country of that sentry up in the tower. You'll be lost there, trying to survive in the ruins of Japan's defeat."

I hoped Mike was right, but I wanted him to shut up. These guys weren't here to talk. Maybe if he didn't make them too mad, they'd just go away.

"You believe too much of what you hear," the guy said. "Propaganda from a government that turned its back on you." He took his eyes off Mike, looked past him for an instant. "You need a lesson," he said. His smirk came back. "Now!"

Suddenly the guy behind us leaped on Mike's back, his forearm went around Mike's neck. I moved to help but the guy on the left grabbed me from behind, pinning my arms, raising his fist to my throat. I felt suffocated. I raised my foot and slammed it down on the top of his just as Mike took a quick step forward and flexed at the waist and the guy riding him went airborne, upside down. He landed in the dirt with a thud and a grunt and an explosion of dust.

I kept struggling as the chief hyena rushed at Mike. But Mike sidestepped him and grabbed his arm as he went by. He twisted it and jammed it high up toward the guy's shoulder blades, forcing him down to his knees.

"Let go of my brother or I'll break this fool's arm," Mike said to my guy. Flying hyena still lay on the ground, groaning, not laughing.

"Tell your friend to let my brother go," Mike said to his guy, putting on more pressure. The friend still had me, but I felt his grip relax. I breathed deep and swallowed hard. Mike forced the arm higher.

"Let him go!" the leader grunted. My guy swore and turned me loose and I spun away to stand near Mike. I felt nauseated. One of them was on his knees, one on his back, and one stood help-lessly, waiting for orders.

"Good," Mike said. He still had his guy down. "Between now and the day you hyenas sail off," he said, breathing hard, "I don't want to see your faces again. If you cause my brother trouble, I'll find you. They'll send you to Japan in a box."

Silence, interrupted only by the sound of breathing, hung over us. A thin layer of ground fog moved in through the dusk.

"Understood?" Mike said.

The guy on his back found his voice. "Understood," he said between quick gulps of air.

"Okay," the other two chorused. Mike backed away and stood side by side with me. Chief guy got to his feet, flexing his arm. He and the guy I'd been dancing with helped up the other one. Without a word they limped off into the gloom.

"Good job, Joe," Mike said, wiping his hands together. I looked at mine. Most of our greasy mud was gone; I pictured it in streaks on the No-Nos' clothes.

"You taught them a lesson," I said.

"But have they learned one?" he said, and I remembered Dad's words about lessons. I remembered what Mom had told us: To lose is to win. Were those guys the winners, then? It didn't feel like it.

Someone walked out of the shadow of our barracks, like a ghost through the mist. He got closer, and I saw he was tall, uniformed, smiling. Sandy.

"Young citizens," he said. He held out his hand, and we shook, Mike first, then me. A family walked by, looking at us curiously. Where had they been a few minutes earlier?

"I'm glad you fellas were able to handle that problem," he said. "I could've stepped in, but then what about the next time? Maybe I wouldn't be around."

"You saw it?" Mike said.

"Nice moves," Sandy said to Mike. "And you were holding your own, Joe."

"He was too strong."

"Three at a time would have been tough," Mike said to me.

"You'll be eighteen soon, Mike?" Sandy said.

"Two weeks."

"Plans?"

"The army." The way Mike said it, so sure, gave me the chills.

"Even after this?" Sandy said, gesturing toward the barracks, the sentry towers, the fences.

Mike nodded. "This is my country too." He smiled. "I *am* a young citizen."

Sandy looked down at Mike's face for a long time, as if he were trying to see behind it, see what made Mike work. "We—the army—could use warriors. You'll make a helluva soldier."

That wasn't what I wanted to hear. I wanted Sandy to tell him he didn't owe anyone anything. But I looked at Mike and knew even Sandy's words wouldn't have made a difference. Maybe Sandy knew it, too.

He took two Baby Ruths from his pocket. "Dessert?" he said, holding them out to us. Mike took one, I took the other. My fingers trembled.

We savored the taste of the candy all the way to the bathroom, where we tried to clean up. Then we trudged back to our room while we talked about what excuse we could make to Mom and Grandmother for our appearance. But they seemed not to notice. Maybe they were used to us looking like hoboes.

My whole body still felt shaky from our meeting with the No-Nos. But I had something to write. I sat on my bunk with my journal and began.

By the time I finished writing of No-Nos—bullies—and me—scared—and Mike—brave—it had grown late. Mike turned out the light and my family got into bed and I listened while Mom talked in the dark of her day, of slicing open a big fish to clean it for cooking and finding its stomach full of maggots.

I closed my eyes and tried to sleep, but my heart still pounded, my ears filled with the night sounds of my family: even breathing and uneven dreams. On the other side of the wall the Suzuki family stirred and coughed and murmured. Outside, ghostly lights reflected off barbed wire, soldiers watched from towers. I fell asleep and dreamed: The No-Nos come back, wounded and maggoty, walking on all fours, fangs glistening, snarling; I'm alone.

I woke in the dark, in the cold, sweating.

By the day of Mike's birthday, he had already made arrangements for his leaving. The army was eager to have him. Sandy had volunteered to drive him to Klamath Falls, where he would take his physical and be sworn in and leave for basic training. But not for three more days. Not until the day after my birthday.

We had a party for both of us on my birthday. We invited Mae and her family and James Ito and his family. No Phillip. The room felt crowded but empty at the same time. They sang "Happy Birthday" twice. We had cake from the mess hall and cold soda pop from Sandy. We opened presents from Mom: clothes for me, stationery and a box of pencils for Mike.

Grandmother gave us small smooth stones with Japanese symbols painted on them: "strength" for Mike, "patience" for me.

"You haven't noticed, Grandmother?" I said.

"What, Joseph?"

"My patience. It's improved."

"The stone is just a reminder," she said. "For when patience becomes a choice again, instead of a sentence. For when we are no longer under the government's thumb."

I couldn't wait for that day. And now I had another reason: to prove to Grandmother that my patience was real. No longer was I the little kid counting days until Christmas.

Mae got me a new pen. The O'Briens sent me another coat, Mike a Saint Christopher medal. He put it on. I imagined it jangling against his dog tags, working its magic. But would it? How many dead soldiers had Saint Christopher's image hanging from their necks? I was thirteen now, but suddenly I felt younger instead of older, on the edge of crying like a baby.

Mom gave us two packages from the unknown person again. Sandy, I decided, but he had never admitted to last year's mystery gifts. I opened mine: *The Adventures of Huckleberry Finn*. Mike unwrapped his: *The Red Badge of Courage*.

Grandmother looked at my book. "I know this one," she said. "Mark Twain." She picked up Mike's, shaking her head. "War," she said.

"It ends okay, Grandmother," Mike said, and gave her a hug.

He was up early the next day, before we could strap him to his bed, before I was all the way awake. He was gone before the sun had cleared the hills, before tears came. I stood with Mom and Grandmother and watched as a tail of dust trailed the jeep out of camp and disappeared.

I felt empty but not hungry. I skipped breakfast and went back to our room. Mike's few belongings were piled in a corner. I looked for his journal; it was gone. I wondered if he had ever written anything in it. Would he now? I got mine from my duffel. I found some words.

PART THREE

Behind thin wood walls,

Freedoms die, pasts dim, but dreams—

Dreams still ramble free!

FOURTEEN

October arrived. The sun continued to shine, but a weeping cloud hung over our family. I finally gave up on a dim hope that the army would send Mike back. He hadn't flunked his physical, he wasn't colorblind or tone-deaf or flat-footed or afraid of loud noises or tough sergeants. If he was any of those things, the army had overlooked them. They'd seen the fire in his eyes.

Dad was still a memory, fading. His photos, in which he never changed, his letters, yellowing on the wall, were all we had of him.

"I've gotten used to Dad's being gone," I told Mom one day as I reread one of his letters for the hundredth time. "He hasn't been here for anything."

I expected Mom to get angry. I was angry at myself for my feelings. Instead she gave me a sad smile. "It's not his fault, Joseph."

"Maybe Mike wouldn't be gone if Dad had been here."

"Put yourself in his place," she said. "From time to time I find myself disappointed in him for being gone. I resent having to fill his shoes while still wearing mine. But then I think about what he has suffered. Imagine how powerless he must feel."

I tried to imagine it. I kicked myself, I wanted to kick the men who were keeping him imprisoned.

There was a knock on our door. I opened it. Mae stood there, smiling with her eyes, trying not to smile with her mouth.

"Come in," I said. The weather had turned cool and windy. I felt a chill. She said hello to Mom, who invited her to sit at the table and have tea. I sat down with them.

"What is it?" I said. Her eyes danced. She was inside, but her cheeks still glowed.

"My family has a sponsor."

Mom smiled. "Wonderful."

I tried smiling. "How?"

"The Quakers helped us."

"Where will you go?" Mom said.

"Oregon," Mae said. "A town called Ontario, like the province in Canada."

"When?" I said.

"Soon," she said. "A week."

A week. She couldn't stop her smile now. I felt myself smiling with her. Something good was happening. And sad. Bittersweet.

"Your father has a job?" Mom said.

"A service station," Mae said. "And we'll be working on the farm where we'll live."

A farm. A real house. A real school. A dad who comes home every night. My dream. I sipped tea and let Mae and Mom talk. Mae's mom came over and the room filled with chatter. Mom wanted to know every detail. I didn't. Finally they left.

I sat there, thinking about asking Mom when she would try

to get us a sponsor. But with Dad locked up and Grandmother a Yes-No, what chance would we have? I put on my coat and left our apartment without saying anything. Patience, I told myself. I walked until my legs grew weary and darkness had fallen over the camp. By the time I returned, Mom had gone to work. Grandmother was waiting for me, waiting to go to dinner. My patience was gone.

"Why hasn't Mom tried to get us a sponsor?" I asked Grandmother as we left the apartment at a slow shuffle.

She took my arm, moving in close to me. I could feel the pressure of her thin fingers through my coat sleeve. She didn't answer at first, and I looked over at her, noticing for the first time that I was taller than she was.

"What makes you think she has not?" she said finally.

"She has?"

"Yes."

"And?"

"It will be difficult while your father is away, she has learned. Not unexpected news."

"Once he is with us?" I said.

"Our prospects improve."

"Yours, too?"

"Yes. I am an old woman. The government might decide I am harmless, even if I answered no on the form."

We were only halfway to the mess hall, late. People were already returning to their barracks. We had only one speed. "Why didn't Mom say anything?"

"She knew that we were not in a good situation. She did not want to raise your hopes and then crush them."

Mom didn't want to raise my hopes, but now I felt them rise a little higher. If Dad returned, if the government forgave Grand-mother her answer, if we found a sponsor, we would have a chance for freedom. Lots of ifs, but even so…I tried to pick up our pace a little. I suddenly realized I was hungry.

The next day I told Sandy about Mae's news. On the following Saturday he asked me if I wanted to get out for a hike before winter set in. I was ready to go before he finished his question. I almost asked if Mae could come, but I changed my mind. I would let her fill someone else's ear with her talk of freedom.

Our first stop was a lake. I was surprised to see it in the mid-dle of this dry country, and more surprised when Sandy told me it was Tule Lake. I'd thought all along that whatever lake had given this place its name had long ago disappeared.

Next we drove to the base of Castle Rock, where we parked the jeep. Sandy knew where he was going—up. Hard work for someone who was used to doing a lot of sitting—me. He picked out a trail and I followed him, sweating, breathing hard. I smelled dust and the sharp perfume of desert plants. The higher we got, the more I could see. I looked down at the camp, the rows of bar-racks stretching into the distance, the barbed wire and guard towers and people moving from place to place like rats in a maze.

We hiked to the peak and sat, sharing sandwiches and candy bars and Cokes near a big white cross some internees had been allowed to erect. The view was beautiful but unsettling. In one direction, camp. In the other, mountains, forests, and thousands of acres of land without fences. But I couldn't go there. My fami-ly couldn't go there.

Halfway back down the rocky trail, Sandy suddenly held up his arm. "Shhh," he hissed.

I stopped just off his right shoulder and looked, not seeing. He snapped open his holster and slowly drew out his pistol and I followed his gaze to the object of his attention: a snake. Eight feet away a fat snake had crawled out onto a flat rock in the middle of the trail and coiled itself in the sun.

"Rattlesnake?" I whispered. As if in answer the snake raised its head and looked at us and gave off a sound I'd heard before only in my imagination. The sound of marbles spilling onto hard ground.

"Big one." Sandy cocked his pistol and leveled it at the snake. But the rattler didn't flinch. Its tongue slipped in and out, testing the air. It didn't know about the power of a gun. But in my imagination I decided the snake was too prideful or maybe too accepting to try to escape. For some reason I thought of Dad, being led away in his pajamas, walking with his head held high. Perhaps this snake believed in the words *shikata ga nai*. But those words had done nothing for Dad. Run, I thought to myself. Slither away.

"Don't shoot him," I said in a loud voice, hoping to warn the snake. It didn't budge.

"No?" Sandy said.

"He can't hurt us from there." I'd read enough of Mike's Zane Grey westerns to know rattlers couldn't fly. I hoped Zane Grey wasn't wrong.

Sandy glanced at me. He smiled. "You're right," he said. Slowly, eyes on the rattler, gun still raised, he bent and picked up a golf ball–size stone. He lobbed it underhand toward the snake's rock. It hit inches away and clattered to the ground. The rattler tensed. Then it dropped its head and uncoiled gracefully and moved away, disappearing into the hillside's cracks and crevices.

Sandy uncocked his pistol and holstered it. I took one last look at the forest in the distance while my heart slowed. Then we continued down.

Later that day I made a journal entry about a snake with dignity, and Dad, who had twice as much. Most of me was proud of the way he was, but a small voice inside me wondered what things would have been like for us if he had been different—not a leader, not a teacher, not honest about who he was or what he'd done. Would he be here with us now? Would we be free?

On the evening before Mae was to leave we brought out the marbles and played until it was too dark to see. She didn't talk at all about her leaving, where they were going, and I was ashamed that I had been jealous of her good fortune. I won one game on my own. She let me win three others. I knew what she was doing—missing on purpose—but I admired how close she came, and I didn't say anything. It was her going-away gift to me.

I had nothing to give her but a poem I had written the night before.

> *Rare pearl, sharpshooter,*
> *Digger of shells, a smile that*
> *Fills an empty heart.*

She took the scrap of lined paper and went to the closest circle of light. Reading the poem shouldn't have taken more than five seconds, but her head stayed down. When she looked up, her eyes were watery, and I had to turn away. First Ray, then Phillip. And now Mae.

I gathered up the marbles—hers and mine—and put them in their sacks. I peered down as Mae came up beside me. In the dark I couldn't make out the circle we'd drawn in the dirt. It had disappeared, just like my small circle of friends.

I walked her back to her barracks. She touched my cheek with her fingers and went inside.

A smiling man in a suit arrived in a dusty black Lincoln the next morning. Mae and her family loaded their belongings in the trunk while some of us—friends from the block, from the White River Valley—helped or watched. It took no time. Then they were inside the big car, saying good-bye through the rolled-down windows. The Lincoln crept away, easing through small clusters of onlookers. I walked along, keeping Mae's face in view as she looked out the back window. Too late, I remembered a promise I hadn't kept: to teach her to whistle. At the gate the car stopped while the guard checked papers and waved them on. Mae's face disappeared in a cloud of dust. I touched my cheek where her fingers had been.

Mike's first letter came the next day. It was short—a half-page of his new stationery—but I made up for it by reading it again and again. He was busy, he said, learning to be a soldier. He'd been assigned to the 442nd Regimental Combat Team, the all-Nisei unit. The army had finally let them hand in the toy guns they'd been issued when they arrived, and entrusted them with real ones. The food reminded him of Tule food, only worse. He'd met other guys from the Seattle area, and when they weren't too tired they had a good time talking about home, about where they might go. France, some of them were guessing. The recruits from Hawaii had come up with the motto for the 442nd: Go for Broke.

It meant putting everything on the line. Mike missed us, he said. Write to me, Joe, he said.

Regimental Combat Team. Go for Broke. Impressive. But I didn't like Mike's being a part of it. I was hoping for White House Guard, or Special Assistant to the General Who Never Leaves the States, or Regimental Latrine Team. I was hoping for a motto like Go for Shelter. But Mike hadn't joined to do any of those things.

I wrote back, telling him about the snake and Mae's leaving. I told him we were doing swell. I pinned his letter to the wall opposite the wall where Dad's letters hung. It looked lonesome by itself, so I cut out articles from newspapers and magazines about American fliers dropping bombs on German cities, American soldiers winning victories in Italy, and pinned them up too. They made me feel better. Maybe if we kept whipping the bad guys, the war would be over before Mike had to go.

After I decorated the wall I sat down and put some thoughts in my journal. They were thoughts about boys going to war who should be home, playing catch with their brothers. They were thoughts about going for broke.

I came home from school one day in mid-October and found Mom and Grandmother talking. Serious faces. Lowered voices.

"A farm worker has died," Mom told me.

"How?" I had heard rumors, but no details.

"A truck overturned," Mom said.

"Bare tires," Grandmother said.

"Bald," Mom said. "People are saying they should have been replaced long ago."

"Someone should do something," Grandmother said.

I pictured a worker crushed under a truck, or thrown, hurtling out and down, like a Canada goose shot from the sky. Part of me was sickened as I thought of the dead man and his family. Part of me was pleased that Mom and Grandmother had brought me into their conversation of grown-up grief.

The next day at breakfast—cold pancakes and Spam—the mess hall was filled with people and talk. I watched with Grand-mother as farm workers sat, as they kept sitting, as their angry voices rose. Word spread. A strike. The farm workers were not going to work until conditions changed.

And they didn't work. For a week. Ten days. Strikebreakers were brought in to finish the harvest. They were paid a dollar an hour instead of what the regular workers made: less than a dollar a day. Anger swirled through the camp. Farm workers. No-Nos. I walked back and forth to school alone, hoping the bad feelings wouldn't spill over on me.

The situation worsened. The people in charge of Tule refused to allow a public funeral for the worker. On the first day of November, I sat outside our barracks and watched as hundreds of people marched past.

"You stay out of the way," Mom said as she left for work. But I followed the noisy crowd to the administration building. Thousands of people were standing in the cold. A man got up and shouted out a speech and read a list of demands. Chanting began. It went on. Soldiers moved in—hundreds of them, armed with machine guns and rifles and bayonets. Some of them looked scared. Some looked angry. All looked ready to shoot.

I moved back. I hurried to our room, wishing for better days. I remembered the last time I'd seen Dad, when he told me not to be afraid. Had he ever imagined anything like this? I was glad that Mae and her family had gotten out.

On November 4th Mom came home early—before supper—from her job. They had shut down her mess hall.

"We will stay here tonight," she said. "Government people have been taking our food and feeding the strikebreakers. People are upset. There have been fights and attacks. Young men are roaming the camp. Soldiers are everywhere. I saw tanks moving."

Grandmother shook her head. We stayed inside. I felt even more like a prisoner. We could hear movement and voices until late. I went to bed hungry.

Our mess hall was open the next morning. But many other things—coal, garbage, warehouses—were shutting down. The strike had spread.

I saw worry in Mom's brave eyes. I felt it, too, like a chill from lingering too long at a drafty window. She made me stay home from school for a few days. When I finally went, the talk was all about the strike and what was going to happen.

A curfew was on, which meant we couldn't be out at night. We could barely be out during the day without soldiers or wardens questioning us. Clubs were being disbanded. Dances, athletics, almost all activities were canceled. They didn't want anyone gathering anywhere. And a stockade—barbed wire and guard towers—was going up around the jail to make room for the leaders of the strike.

The camp was nearly paralyzed. The boredom I'd felt before was nothing like this. There was little to do but be scared. Days grew darker and colder. Snow fell. We spent more and more time in our room, dressed in sweaters and coats, trying to get by with the little coal we could get. I wanted more than ever to be out.

Letters from Mike lifted my spirits. I pinned them up, along with new articles on the war in Europe. I inspired Grandmother, who tacked up articles of her own next to Dad's letters. She had clipped them from the Seattle newspapers before we'd left home, and saved them, like a cop saving the confessions of criminals. Those articles and their headlines had done as much as anything to guarantee we'd end up at Tule Lake and places like it.

One article talked about raids on "Jap sympathizers" in the Seattle area and elsewhere. In another the head of Washington State's American Legion said all Issei should be put in concentration camps. An article in the *Seattle Times* headlined ARROWS OF FIRE told the tall tale of arrow-shaped fires near Port Angeles directing Japanese planes to their target—Seattle. When it was later discovered that the fires had been started by loggers burning slash, the *Times* didn't bother to retract the story. Grandmother kept clipping and saving articles, even after we were locked up. Her favorite contained a quote from General DeWitt, to explain his support of internment: "A Jap's a Jap." Grandmother called him General Dimwit.

Thanksgiving came. People puzzled over what to be thankful for. Grandmother invited Mr. and Mrs. Terada to our room for tea and cookies. They were grateful to be with us. I was thankful to have them.

Christmas slipped past. Letters came from Mike and Dad, worried about what was happening at Tule. I worried more about them. I wrote back that we were safe.

The new year—1944—arrived. My wall filled with news of Allied struggles in Italy. One article told of a bloody battle at a place called Cassino, where Japanese Americans from Hawaii were making an "outstanding contribution." Among other things, they were using their baseball skills to fire grenades at German positions, knocking the Nazis back on their heels. I prayed for a quick victory—in the battle and in the war. Mike wanted to prove his loyalty. He didn't have to prove anything to me.

The government reinstituted the draft for Japanese American citizens in good standing. Which meant Yes-Yes Nisei would have to serve in the army even if they didn't volunteer. Which brought more hard feelings and arguments and trouble to Tule. If that were possible.

Mike was still training in the States—a place called Camp Shelby in Mississippi—but itching for a fight. The combat team had yet to see combat.

The days grew longer and warmer as spring approached. People returned to the farms. The strike had ended but the camp turned uglier, with No-Nos gloating because they wouldn't be drafted and demanding the camp for themselves. I would have gladly given it to them.

A letter came from Mike. He had gotten orders. Overseas. He didn't know where. But he had a two-week furlough. He was coming to see us, to say good-bye. Bittersweet.

I hung around the gate on the day he was to arrive. When I saw dust rising far down the road and the dark shape of a bus appeared and grew larger, my heart stalled.

The gate opened, the bus growled through it and stopped. I hurried to the door. Two white soldiers got off—MPs returning from Klamath Falls. Then another soldier, one I hardly recognized in his uniform and cap, stepped off. His face was dark and angled and older, his shoulders had broadened. But he knew me.

Before I could move, he'd crossed the space between us and scooped me up as if I were a little kid and wrapped me in a big bear hug.

"That's the last time I'll be able to do that," Mike said, and I got this sinking feeling in my chest as he set me down. I must have given him a worried look.

"You're getting too big," he said. "Next time you can pick me up." He smiled, wide and easy.

"Okay," I said, although I hadn't grown that much.

"Where's Mom?" he said. "Grandmother?"

"Mom's working," I said. "She'll be off soon. Grandmother's having a little trouble walking. She's waiting to see you in the room." I looked at him. A darker, smaller version of Sandy. Handsome. Dashing. Heroic. Things I'd once thought were important. But seeing Mike in uniform reminded me of other things. Years of not seeing him. Far-off bloody battles. Death. I should have reached across the table on registration day and changed his answers to no-no.

"Grandmother's sourness has settled in her legs." He picked up his bag and put his arm around me and smiled again. We started for the barracks and for a moment everything seemed better.

It didn't stay that way long.

Mike was happy to hang around with us that day and the next. Happy to stay in our room, go to the mess hall, go to Mom's work so she could show him off to her friends. Go to the canteen with me.

But he was used to freedom now. On the third day he decided

he wanted to hike to the farms. "I want to pretend I'm not under the government's thumb for a little while," he said.

I left school at noon. I had this idea that the guards would let me go with him. A crazy idea. We got as far as the gate. That was it. They wouldn't even let Mike out. "Not without an escort," an MP said. I couldn't believe it.

"I'm in the army," Mike said. "Same as you. I arrived without an escort. When I leave here, I'll leave without one. I'll be going to fight the war without one."

"Sorry," the guy said. He looked as if he was.

"What if I put on my uniform?"

"Sorry," the MP repeated. "Regulations."

Mike gave him a look, and for a minute I was afraid there was going to be trouble. But Mike turned and started away. "C'mon, Joe," he said.

"Maybe Sandy can do something," I said.

"Sandy has a big heart, but he's a sergeant," Mike said. "Those orders were cooked up by someone with a small mind but lots of brass. Sandy can't do anything about it."

I didn't argue. Mike was right. We went back to the room, where Grandmother was making flowers. Her fingers danced through a pile of shells, searching for the perfect ones. I had made it hard for her; I hadn't gathered any since Mae had left.

"I thought you were going for a walk, Michael," she said.

"I changed my mind."

"Oh?" She put down the shells and gave him a long look.

"They won't let him go," I said. "Not without a baby-sitter." I told her what had happened, while Mike stood at the window, looking out at dirt and guard towers and fences. She shook her head and her jaw slid out and set. I had second thoughts about my decision to tell her. Mike's answer might have been better.

"You are an American," she said to Mike's back. "A *cit-i-zen*." She stretched out the word like a snake uncoiling and skimming across a warm rock. "You have shown what that means by joining the army. Who knows what that decision will cost you?"

"It's going to cost *them*," Mike said, turning toward us. "The Nazis will pay."

"And who else?" Grandmother said. I couldn't help wondering along with her. Who else? The question took my breath away.

Mike sidestepped it with a shrug. "Don't worry."

But I did worry. I escaped to my journal. I wrote about the way Mike looked in his uniform, and fences, and Sandy, and long-ago trains. I wrote about a wish: Mike and Sandy going to war together. I added a poem.

> *A loyal heart beats,*
> *Unseen, beneath khaki skin.*
> *Can none hear it sing?*

The next day Sandy took us through the gate. He drove us to where he and I had gone before: Tule Lake, Castle Rock. We walked the same trail, but it wasn't the same. Mike took it all in, but he was quiet. And I wasn't much company. My mind was already on his leaving. When we got to the top, he wandered off by himself and sat down on a slab of stone and stared off toward the trees and Mount Shasta in the distance as if we weren't there.

"I have to be going soon, too," Sandy told me.

"Where?"

"The war. They figure I've seen enough of this one."

"You'll have to fight?"

"It's why I joined."

"Can you go where Mike goes? Look after him, kind of?"

"I'd like to, Joe. But I've got no say. And I don't know where Mike's going, but I'm guessing Europe. I'm heading in the other direction."

"To fight Japan?"

Sandy nodded.

"And Mike will be fighting the Nazis?"

"He's a tough guy. I wouldn't want to be in their boots."

Sandy was right. Mike was tough. But did that matter to a bullet?

We started back down. I took the lead, looking for snakes, hoping for something to change the feeling in the air, in me. But there were no snakes. Nothing changed.

When I left for school the next day Mike was still in bed. When I got back he was waiting outside for me. He had my baseball and a couple of old battered gloves he'd borrowed from one of our neighbors. We tossed the ball back and forth, warming up, moving farther and farther apart, throwing harder and harder. The ball stung my hand through the thin leather, but I didn't complain, I didn't want to quit.

When we finally did, I went in and got my marbles. We found a spot in the shade where Mae and I had played a thousand games, but there wasn't a trace of us left in the soft dirt. I drew a circle and we divvied up the marbles. I let Mike have the ones Ray had given me, but they weren't magic, and he was rusty. I beat him four straight. He didn't seem to mind, though. He concentrated harder and edged me in the fifth game and I was glad. If I'd let him win, he would have guessed it.

Mom returned from work. We went to supper. When we came back to our room, Mike had an announcement: He wasn't going to stay as long as he'd planned. He was leaving the next day. He loved us, he said, but he just had to leave.

I didn't have to ask why. I understood how it must feel to have some freedom again and then have it torn away. Once he'd told us, and we'd all stood in the middle of the little room and held each other, and he'd gone outside for some air, Grandmother summed it up. "Government," she said.

"Vermin," Mom said. I smiled through my tears.

FIFTEEN

When I woke up the next morning, Mike was in his uniform, sitting on the edge of his cot, looking at me. Mom stood near the door, her hands clasped in front of her, as if she didn't know what else to do with them. She was waiting. I thought of the other shoe. Grandmother sat at the table, reading the *San Francisco Chronicle*.

"I've gotta go, Joe."

"When?"

"Now. Early bus."

"Some people are predicting an Allied invasion soon," Grandmother said, eyes on the paper. "France, possibly. A chance for the Nazis to look death in the face." I knew what she was doing. I didn't want to think about what was happening right here, in this room, either.

"Maybe they won't like its looks," Mom said.

Grandmother glanced at Mike. "Maybe they will surrender."

"I hope I'm there to see it," he said. He stood, put on his cap, grabbed his bag.

Mom put her arms around him. "We would love you to stay longer." She had been strong, always. Now her face—a child's—begged him to reconsider.

He smiled, wet-eyed. "I can't, Mom."

"No," she said. She let him go and he bent and hugged Grandmother.

By the time he got to the door I was out of bed and in my pants and shirt. I wedged on my shoes and caught up to him. "I'll walk with you," I said. I wanted to see him for a while longer. I wanted to leave Mom's brave, sad face behind.

He nodded and gave Mom and Grandmother a little salute and we stepped into the cool morning air. We headed for the gate, Mike walking tall. I felt taller too, just walking beside him. People were looking at us, smiling, nodding, wishing him good luck. An old man said something to him in Japanese and Mike said, "Thank you, Grandfather."

"Write to us, Michael," Mom called, and he turned back and gave her a thumbs-up. Grandmother stood next to her, a handkerchief at her face. She offered it to Mom, who shook her head. She wiped at her cheek with the back of her hand.

The bus was waiting, its engine muttering and exhaling blue exhaust. The driver climbed on, glanced at his watch, and gave Mike a look. It was time. Mike hugged me tight, lifting me off the ground once more. Then he was up the steps and out of sight. I waited for him to appear at one of the windows but he must have sat on the other side, where I couldn't see him. I didn't go check. I had tears in my eyes. Maybe he did, too.

I went back to our room. Mom and Grandmother were both gone. School could wait. I got out my journal and thought about

Mike. I wrote of his leaving early because staying was too painful. I wrote of Mom's eyes melting like wax.

The day felt empty until I went to our block manager to check for mail. A letter had arrived from Mae. The people in Ontario were mostly nice—Japanese and non-Japanese. The area was dry and hot—not like Seattle—but they had a house to live in; her father had a job. She had made a friend—a Japanese American girl—and Mae was trying to teach her to play marbles. "But it isn't the same," Mae said. "I don't miss Tule Lake, but I miss you." I read those words over and over. She said she hoped my family would also get sponsored by someone in Ontario. She was talking with her parents about it.

The idea sounded good to me, although I couldn't see it working soon. Grandmother may have been right: She was old; maybe the government would consider her harmless. But still she was a Yes-No and Dad was a prisoner, a threat.

But maybe Mike would balance off at least one of those. I shelved the thought in the back of my brain, where I kept most of my hopes. I hadn't given up on them, but it didn't do me any good to have them up front, where they might get in the way of real life. I had been away from home, locked up, for two years already. I wasn't going to hold my breath waiting for something good to happen.

After school I tossed around the baseball with a couple of younger boys from the next barracks. Then I dug a bag of shells for Grandmother. She was spending the afternoon alone in our room, filling it with sighs. I would give her something to do. She was pleased; she said she would take a gift of flowers to Mrs. Terada.

That night I had a hard time sleeping. Sometime late or early— the room was midnight-dark—I woke to a noise. The click of a latch, a door opening, closing again. Mom or Grandmother, I decided, going to the bathroom, coming back. But I peered toward their cots and even in the dark I could see their outlines, motionless except for the push and pull of their breathing. I looked toward the door. Had someone been in the room? Were they still here? Had I dreamed it?

In front of the door was a shape, standing, moving, turning in one direction then another. I didn't know what to do. Keep quiet? Yell? What would Mike do? Leap up, my heart was telling me, but I didn't do that either. I lay there, frozen, as the form—a man, I decided—moved away from the door and approached our cots.

Walking soundlessly, he came closer, paused, then veered toward me. I closed my eyes. What could he want?

I smelled something. Familiar, but not familiar in this room. Shaving lotion. Old Spice. What was Sandy doing here? Had he come to say good-bye? But Sandy wouldn't sneak into our room in the middle of the night.

I felt fingers—not Sandy's sausage-size ones—on my cheek. I tried not to flinch. Next would they move to my neck? I heard the man make a soft noise in his throat—a sob—and I sensed him lowering himself, crouching next to me.

Suddenly a dam burst in the back of my brain. A wall of hope surged past it. "Dad?" I said.

His arms went around me, mine around him, our cheeks came together, wet. "Yes," he said, lifting me, standing, holding me off the floor. "Yes, my big son!"

"Dad!" I shouted. The light went on, Mom and Grandmother

hurried to us and wrapped their arms around us and we stood, holding on in the middle of our ugly little room that instantly looked beautiful to me. Tears fell like warm rain. I studied my father's face—older, thinner, shadowed, but still his face. Still him.

We sat down around the little table and talked, sometimes all at once. Dad hadn't expected his release, so he couldn't write to tell us. He'd come by train and bus with some other men and an MP. Once at Tule Lake, he'd had to ask directions of the gate guard, then knock on an apartment door a couple of barracks away and wake up someone before he could find us.

I couldn't believe how a day that had started off so bad had ended up so good. But why couldn't Mike have lasted one more day? Why couldn't Dad have come a day earlier? *Government,* I thought.

We told Dad about Mike's leaving, why he left. His eyes lost some of their spark. He went to the window and stared off into the night, as if he were trying to catch sight of someone disappearing in the distance. We waited. He came back, trying to smile. He hugged me again, double tight, as if he could make up for not seeing his other son.

"I will enjoy the family I have here," he said. "I will enjoy Michael when he returns."

I heard the resignation in his voice. I also heard the strength. He was trying to bear up under one more burden, to make peace with the situation he'd found: a gain, a loss. Could I be like him? I wondered. Was I still the same person who had felt so much pain when Dad had been stolen from us, when we'd left our home, left Ray, when Phillip, then Mike, then Mae, had slipped away?

I didn't think so. But had I grown up? Or just grown numb? Did it matter? I decided I would try to be more like Dad. And Mom, too. *Shikata ga nai.*

We said a prayer for Mike, for us. We went to bed. My parents moved their cots close together and talked long after I turned off the light. I fell asleep to the comforting sound of their voices.

I woke up late the next morning. And alone. For an instant I was afraid the night before had been one of those realistic dreams in which something wonderful happens and you wake up the next morning bitterly disappointed. But I saw Dad's suitcase, his clothes hung over a bench, and I knew it had really happened. I had something to write about, and I did.

Mom and Dad (I loved being able to string those words together) had left me a note. They were walking. Grandmother was visiting Mrs. Nomura. When they came back, we went to breakfast. A lot of people came up to say hello to Dad, to say how happy they were to meet him or see him again after all this time. Among them were Mr. and Mrs. Yano and their two sons. I remembered a time much earlier, when those boys, smaller and still free, had stood at our door with their parents.

I wondered how much things would change now that Dad was with us, now that he wasn't a prisoner. Was there a chance we could get our freedom?

Mom went to work late. I went to school late. Mrs. Berger made me write an essay on why I was grateful to have my dad back. It wasn't easy. The reasons didn't fit inside the boundaries of words. And every time I thought about how grateful I was to have him back, I thought about all the time he'd been away, all the things I'd missed, he'd missed, we'd missed. He'd been gone for two and a half years. Was I supposed to be grateful for that? I remembered my resolution to be more like him.

Just after sundown Dad and I walked to the fence. He was used to fences, he'd told us, but as we stood looking past the barbed wire at the flatlands and hills around us, I felt ashamed. I felt as if someone important had dropped in unannounced and found me living in a hobo shack surrounded by rusting washing machines and iceboxes and skinny, bad-tempered dogs chewing on brined liver.

The sky darkened over the hills. The first star—a planet, maybe—twinkled to life. I had many wishes, but only three big ones. One of them—Dad's return—had just been granted. Another—that we would get out of Tule, go to a place where we could be free—would have to happen on its own. The third one—Mike's safe return—would get all of my attention from now on. That was the wish I hung on that first star.

I felt Dad's eyes on me and I moved closer to him.

"Did you wish?" he said. He smiled. I had been afraid his smile would come only rarely, like new needles on a fir.

"Yes," I said.

"May I guess?"

"You already know."

The air had gotten cooler. He put his arm around my shoulders. "Mike?"

I nodded, wondering where he was. On a train, probably. Alone. Not knowing Dad was with us, not knowing how close they'd come to seeing each other. I thought of making another wish: that I could turn back time, that I could beg Mike to stay another day. But I couldn't afford wasted wishes.

"Mine, too," Dad said. "I may come out here every night and make that wish. And when I'm not here, I will be asking help from Jesus or Buddha or whoever happens to be listening."

"One of my wishes was answered," I said.

Dad pulled me closer to him. He still felt strong. "One of mine, also," he said. "I am so happy to be with you again."

He asked me about my journal, whether I'd been keeping one. I told him yes, but hoped he wouldn't ask to see it, and he didn't. Still, he looked pleased when I got it out of my bag later that night, when I sat and struggled with sleepiness and managed to get something written.

SIXTEEN

Dad knew one of the farm foremen. He was able to land a job a few days after he arrived, which meant a little more money for us. Not much else changed, but I wasn't disappointed. Not yet. I was learning patience. And with him around, every day seemed brighter, as if a layer of clouds had burned away.

Our days settled into a routine. Dad and Mom going off to work, Grandmother going off to visit or, if her legs were bothering her, staying in the room and reading a newspaper or working on her flowers. Me going off to school.

Dad came home tired every day, but he looked healthier. He gained weight. At day's end he would walk, sometimes alone, sometimes with me or me and Mom. Sometimes Grandmother would go. We always stopped at the fence and paid our respects to the sunset, the first star.

I wrote to Mike. Dad and Mom had already written to tell him of Dad's homecoming, but they hadn't told him of the timing. I, too, was careful not to let him know he and Dad had come within hours of seeing each other. I had told Grandmother why Mike wasn't allowed to go through the gate, and what good had it done? He heard the out-loud anger, the resentment in my voice. And she became upset. Had our words crept inside his head, giving him thoughts of leaving us early? And sharing with Mike this other burden—the reunion, barely missed—would relieve me but weigh on him. He already had much on his shoulders.

I wrote to Mae and told her where Mike might be going, that we hadn't heard from him yet. I said to find us a sponsor, that my marbles were getting dusty.

A letter came from Mike. We saved it, unopened, until we were all together that night, then sat at the table and listened as Mom read it. Hitler was still in business, Mike said. The 442nd was shipping out the next day, destination somewhere in Europe. They were sailing from an East Coast port, crossing the Atlantic. France was still a possibility, he said, but it was probably too early for France. North Africa had been a choice, but North Africa was ours now. Italy had become the betting favorite. He missed us. "I'll keep my helmet on, Mom," he said. He didn't say anything to Dad. He was moving too fast for our letters to catch him.

One evening toward the end of May, Dad came home late. He'd been walking, he said. His face was dark from sun. And something else.

"What is it, Tomio?" Mom said.

"A man—one of the men I work with—was shot today," he said. "The guard thought he was trying to escape through the gate. He was only trying to catch up to the truck."

"He is dead?" Grandmother said.

"In the hospital," Dad said. "Not good." The hospital. I felt sorry for the man. Grandmother had gotten a high fever once and refused to go to the camp hospital. "A stop on the way to the cemetery," she said.

The next day word spread through Tule. The man—Shoichi James Okamoto—was dead. Unrest boiled up once again. Because internee leaders demanded an investigation, one was done. When it was finished, the guard was found blameless, except for misuse of government property—the bullet. He was fined a dollar.

June arrived. School got out. More time on my hands. I tried to pass it by playing baseball—I hadn't touched a basketball since my last day at Ray's house—or going on walks, reading the newspapers, catching up on things with Dad. But it was mostly one-way. He wanted to talk about what I'd been doing, what Mike and I had done before Mike joined the army. Dad was hungry for what he'd missed in the years he was gone. I asked him questions, but his answers were short. He didn't like talking about his days in Montana and New Mexico.

I spent a lot of time thinking about Mike, wondering where he was, how he was, and wishing there was some way I could find out. But the newspapers didn't say anything about the 442nd. I had to guess, and my guessing always put him in the middle of some terrible battle where men on both sides fell like ripening cherries in a hailstorm. So when I learned of D-day—the Allied invasion of France on June 6th—I pictured Mike coming ashore on the bloody beaches of Normandy, bullets whistling past his head, bombs blowing geysers of sand and water high above him.

My imagination cursed me to long days of wanting to read the newspapers and magazines but not wanting to read them, waiting for the mail but not wanting to look at it. And dreading the sight of the Western Union couriers with their telegrams of tears, the army cars with their messengers of loss. I'd seen the gold stars on flags hanging in barracks windows. Those gold stars meant a mom had lost a son in the war. I couldn't stand the thought of one of those flags hanging in our window.

I usually read the *San Francisco Chronicle* or *Life* magazine. Both of them were for sale at the canteen. But one day Grandmother came home from her friend Mrs. Takazaki's with pieces of a Honolulu newspaper. Mrs. Takazaki had a niece in Hawaii, where there were many Japanese Americans, and a nephew in the 100th Battalion, an all-Nisei unit of soldiers from Hawaii. Mrs. Takazaki's niece sent her aunt articles from the Honolulu newspapers whenever there was news of the 100th or the other army unit that had a big share of Japanese Americans from Hawaii—the 442nd.

Grandmother called me to the table and we sat and traded articles back and forth. The paper was more than a week old, but I found reports on the 100th and the 442nd. The 100th—the Purple Heart Battalion, it was called, because of all the casualties it had suffered—was battling its way through Italy. The 442nd was still at sea, official destination unknown.

I felt better knowing that someone was paying attention to the Nisei soldiers, that I'd be able to see stories—late or not—on what they were doing. Mrs. Takazaki had promised to share whatever she got with us. And Grandmother said Mrs. Nomura's granddaughter in Illinois would send reports from her newspapers. "The papers on the other side of the country treat our soldiers like citizens," Grandmother said.

I got a letter from Ray. I tried to picture his face. I couldn't. How long had it been since I last saw him? How much had he changed? Was he as tall as a man now? "I went by your old house," he wrote. "A new family was there, working in the yard. I saw a mom and dad and two boys. I couldn't talk to them. I had to leave." I felt hollow, suddenly. "All for one," he said at the end.

I wrote back with my news and "One for all." I put Ray's letter in my duffel with the rest. I didn't say anything to my family. Ray had shared his burden with me. Two of us were enough to carry it.

Sandy knocked on our door one evening after supper. I introduced him to Dad, who said he was glad to meet him and looked like he meant it. Mom must have told him of Sandy's kindnesses. Even Grandmother smiled. She offered him a chair, and he sat on its edge, dangling his cap between his knees, kneading it nervously with his big fingers.

"I'm leaving tomorrow," he said.

"For good?" I said.

He nodded and looked at my parents. "Thanks for letting me spend time with your sons." He looked at Grandmother. "With your grandsons. I know you're all proud of them. You should be." My eyes clouded over. "It's been a privilege knowing you folks. I wish we could've met under different circumstances."

"Thank you for all you have done," Dad said.

Sandy got to his feet and took a piece of paper from his pocket. "This is my address, in case you'd care to write me. I'd love hearing from any of you." He handed me the paper and walked to the door.

"Wait," I said. I went to my duffel and took out my journal and tore out a back page. On it I had written something for him.

Thinking of the sea,
Of what lies across it, he
Still finds time for me.

I gave him the page. "Thanks," I said. "For everything."

He read the poem, smiling, nodding. "This is great," he said. "Great." He cleared his throat. "Mind if I share it?"

"No," I said.

"She'll love it," he said, and I knew who he meant. "I'd like to see more of your writing sometime, Mr. Twain."

"Okay," I said. We shook, my hand disappearing in his one last time. I thought about asking him if he'd given Mike and me the books. I wanted to thank him. But some questions are better left unasked. And I wasn't sure I could use my voice. "I'll miss you," I managed.

"Take care, Joe." He gave me a hug, a bone-crusher. I smelled Old Spice.

"We will pray for you," Mom said, and I was glad to hear her words. We had drifted away from church, but Mom hadn't given up on prayer. Now we had two soldiers who needed watching over, and I was sure Mom's prayers would be much more powerful than mine.

"Thanks, Mrs. Hanada." Sandy opened the door and walked out into the night.

Grandmother didn't say *government.*

A letter came from Mike. He was okay, at least when he wrote the letter. I thought of the faraway stars, how their light could reach us long after they had died out. I pushed the thought away.

He hadn't been involved in the invasion of Normandy, after all. "We landed in Naples, Italy," he said, "then arrived in a place called Anzio two days too late to help kick the Nazis out of Rome." The 442nd was going to be joined by the 100th Battalion, he said. Then they were going to go to war. "Sorry I missed you, Dad," he wrote at the end. "But I'm glad you're with the rest of the family at last. I'll see you after we're done burying Mr. Mustache. Soon."

I reread Mike's letter, trying to make sense of it, wishing for a map. What I did know was he was going to be fighting now, in the thick of things. And I knew if I read any accounts of the Purple Heart Battalion—the 100th—Mike's battalion, the 3rd Battalion of the 442nd Regimental Combat Team, would be nearby.

Unrest continued at Tule Lake. Every day I watched as unhappy residents and grim-faced soldiers eyed one another with suspicion. Everyone wanted to be somewhere else, but most of us had nowhere to go. And according to what we had heard and read, many of our old neighbors didn't want us back.

July began with a murder. A man was stabbed to death outside a barracks. Tension in the camp swept higher. The *Chronicle* reported it, but barely. An alien, they called him, as if he didn't matter. Day after day I checked the newspaper's lists of war casualties—wounded, dead, missing, imprisoned. I knew there were Japanese Americans dying and wounded and missing and imprisoned, but I didn't see any Japanese names. It was as if they too didn't matter.

Another letter came from Mike. He joked about the food, the

bad weather, the latrines, the 100th Battalion guys and their pidgin that no one could understand. "Those guys have been over here a long time, fighting, suffering casualties. They don't think much of us newcomers. So now we have to prove ourselves to our own people, too." Other than that, he didn't talk about the war. I looked between the lines. My imagination took me to scary places. I put his letter on the wall, thankful for it.

I asked my parents and Grandmother if they knew where I might find a map of Europe, or at least Italy. The library, Mom thought. The canteen, Dad suggested.

Grandmother brought me a map. Another friend of hers gave it to her. A Gold Star Mom. She didn't need the map any longer. It was frayed at the folds and discolored and wrinkled, as if someone had been studying it with their fingers, but all the countries of Europe were there. I spread it out on the table and Grandmother and I studied and pointed and guessed for a long time, as if we were planning a wonderful vacation and just need-ed to decide where on Italy's boot we should go. My parents came home, and we all looked at the map together as if we were hypnotized, as if we expected to see a miniature version of Mike moving across its surface, shouldering a gun, waving up at us.

That night Mom and Dad borrowed a neighbor's chessboard and played chess while Grandmother read an old *Life* magazine that contained a photo of a Nisei soldier who had been blinded by the explosion of a mine while fighting in Italy. An American hero, the magazine called him. I sat on my cot and puzzled over entries for my journal. And wrote. And puzzled. Mike was already a hero. He didn't have to prove it by being blinded. Or worse. He didn't have to prove it to me.

More days passed. I tried to stay out of the sun, I waited for mail. I read newspapers, skipping over headlines that screamed *Jap*, squirming at editorial-page cartoons that showed a bucktoothed, squinty-eyed enemy. I remembered a lifetime earlier, when someone had left a similar drawing on my desk at school.

Honolulu papers had some news of the Nisei, but those papers were old. So were the clippings sent by Molly Nomura. The *Newell Star* had stories that relied on other papers and letters and rumors, and suffered from censorship. West Coast papers had almost nothing in them about Japanese American soldiers. Finally, the July 23, 1944, edition of the *Chronicle* had something. A report from the Italian front headlined DOWN FROM THE HILLS talked about the 100th Battalion, that it *included* some Japanese Americans, that the battalion had come out of the hills and captured the town of Livorno. I unfolded the map and found Livorno on Italy's coast. It looked close to France, close to where the Nazi army would run out of room to backpedal and begin fighting like a cornered pack of hyenas.

August arrived. Harvest began. Headlines in the *Chronicle* said GREATEST GAINS SINCE INVASION. An article reported that a Pennsylvania man who had correctly predicted June 6th as D-day was now predicting that Germany would stop fighting on August 4th. I prayed he was right.

In the comics Superman was making short work of some bad guys. I wished he were real, that he could wipe out the bad guys who had started this war. But he wasn't real. And August 4th came and went with Germany still fighting. Prayers and wishes—neither one was working.

Letters arrived.

One from Mike. It was short and scribbled and the paper was smeared with dirt. I pictured him writing, sitting under the lip of a foxhole. He told us more jokes. They were empty, but we didn't care. He was still writing. He was still alive. The letter went on the wall.

One from Mae. "My parents are talking to people about sponsorships for your family."

"Don't get your hopes too high," Dad said. But he looked hopeful.

"Because of me," Grandmother said. "Because I answered yes-no."

"Not because of you," Dad told her. "Because of me. Because it is a difficult process. But it is kind of Mae's family to speak for us."

One from Ray, hoping the war would be over soon so Mike could come back, so we could return to the White River Valley. He didn't say anything about people there not wanting us— all for one, he said—but I was getting good at reading between the lines.

I wrote back to them. One for all, I told Ray, wondering if I would ever see him again. His letter went in my bag with the rest of my White River Valley life. I pinned Mae's letter to the wall.

I kept reading every newspaper I could find, every article Grandmother brought home. There was one about General DeWitt getting a secret assignment, about him being the one who had ordered our internment.

"Dimwit," Grandmother said. "I would like to choose his secret assignment."

I kept reading, day after day. The Allies were moving toward Paris, Hitler was on the run. But as far as I knew, Mike was still in Italy. Those cornered hyenas were making a stand.

I kept looking, and General Eisenhower's army—not General Clark's, which included the 442nd—continued moving across France. Maps of France appeared on the front pages. Allies were in sight of the Eiffel Tower. Then entering Paris. But where was Mike?

I studied the map, the Honolulu papers, the clippings from Illinois. I waited for a letter, hoping. I walked to the fence with Dad and wished on stars. I always made the same wish. So did he. Mom preferred praying. I prayed that her powerful prayers were working. Grandmother did her part and busied herself by reading and talking.

Finally, in the first week of September, another letter came from Mike. He wasn't supposed to tell us where he was but he did anyway. Italy, still, but he didn't know for how long. He was keeping his helmet on. He missed us.

School started again, and I was grateful. It gave me something to think about besides Mike. Dad was busy with the harvest, Mom with her job, Grandmother with her friends. We didn't talk about Mike much, but he was always in our hearts. At night, when the lights were out and my parents had quit murmuring to each other and Grandmother had begun to snore softly, I lay with my eyes closed and imagined him in the room, drifting off to sleep. I heard his breathing slow and deepen and settle into a rhythm. I tried to match it as I lay on my side and closed my eyes and pictured him in a cot next to me, close enough to touch.

September ended with a sigh. We remembered Mike's birthday by standing at the fence—my parents, Grandmother, and me—and talking about him into the night. When my birthday arrived, Mom and Dad gave me a basketball, Grandmother gave me a new map of Europe. They sang "Happy Birthday"—a sad and lonely-voiced version until the Suzuki family joined in through the wall. We laughed, and invited them over for cake, but part of me still felt resentful that we had so little privacy. *Shikata ga nai*, I told myself.

Our next letter from Mike was dated September 25th. "A bunch of new guys have come in," he said, "to replace the Hawaiian guys who wandered off in search of poi and pine-apple." I didn't get it at first.

"He means they have lost men." Dad's voice sounded raspy. "It is supposed to be lighthearted."

Lighthearted. Maybe. But not funny. It was the first time he'd talked about losing men, and I didn't like it.

The 442nd was leaving Italy, Mike said, shipping out, going to a new place to play tag with the Nazis. He didn't know where. It was a secret, but rumors were flying. The Hawaiians were bet-ting on France, and Mike said he wouldn't want to bet against anyone who lived by the motto Go for Broke. He guessed they were right. I didn't know whether to be glad or upset that they were leaving Italy. Maybe they were going somewhere safer. Maybe they weren't.

That night I studied the newspaper; I pored over the new map until it grew wrinkles and ridges of its own. Mike thought France this time, but where? Paris was liberated and safe—a good place—but they wouldn't need him in Paris. Battles were raging elsewhere. There were stories of super armies guarding

Germany, Nazi death camps. It was October now. Mike could be up to his neck in war.

I went to the fence with Dad, I went for a walk, I came back and wrote in my journal of Mike's funny stories of war that made no one laugh, and the scary accounts we read elsewhere.

What if the stories
Are just tales, like men from Mars,
Beasts under a bed?

SEVENTEEN

The destination of the 442nd really *was* a secret. The newspapers, even those from Hawaii, lost track of the Nisei, as if they'd not just left Italy but sailed away from the planet. We waited for a letter from Mike, clippings from Molly Nomura. Nothing came. I read what was there and looked at the map and tried to imagine where Mike might fit into the puzzle. I liked to picture him on a beach on the French Riviera, lying in the sun, looking for enemy submarines, with no Nazis within a hundred miles.

October inched by. We still didn't hear from Mike. The papers stayed silent on Nisei soldiers. But the *Chronicle* brought us news from Seattle. Farmers in the White River Valley had started an anti-Nisei organization called the Remember Pearl Harbor League. They wanted to keep evacuated Japanese Americans from returning.

I thought of the Spooners. They wouldn't have joined. I pictured them standing up at meetings of the Remember Pearl Harbor

League and arguing against the hate tactics of that crowd. How many others would have stood with them?

The *Chronicle* said that Dillon Myer, the head of the Relocation Authority, met with the leader of the group to remind them that returning Japanese American veterans were citizens and that there were twelve thousand Japanese Americans fighting. "In one relocation center recently we had forty-six Gold Star Mothers whose sons had been killed in action," he said. "In one battalion there were fifty-four holders of Silver Stars and more than one thousand men with Purple Hearts." I wondered if the nice words had changed anyone's mind. I had a feeling we wouldn't be returning to our valley.

At last a letter came from Mike. He couldn't tell us where he was, but they'd traveled a thousand miles by truck to get there, and he could practically see Germany. "It's cold here," he wrote, "and the rain refuses to stop. The overcoats they issued us at first were too big, so they got us some WAC coats. Just right."

For the first time he mentioned the fighting, and after my picturing him on a quiet beach, his words gave me a chill. It was fierce, he said, made worse by the weather. I could see signs of it on his stationery and envelope—water marks, smudges of dried mud, a dirty half-thumbprint. Letters were still coming through, he said, and the guys were glad to get them. "But sometimes the support people risk their lives to get letters to the frontline guys and then have to take them back because the guys they were meant for have been killed." Was he trying to say something without saying it? This time I didn't want to read between the lines.

At the end of his letter he wrote something for me. "Joe," he said, "we're going to get this thing over with before you have to

put on a uniform. But I want you to forget about the army, anyway. Try hard in school. Go to college. Show everyone what a
good writer Joe Hanada is. Make something wonderful of yourself. Make all this worthwhile. And keep those marbles handy.
I'll be ready for a rematch when I come home." That's what I
wanted. Mike to come home. What I didn't want was his advice.
I didn't like the way it felt: final.

The newspapers became my bible. I read them and studied
the map and talked big, filling in gaps with false courage. "I
bet the Nazis are running scared," I'd say, and the family would
nod and go along. Over the next days, while other kids thought
about school and Halloween and an upcoming dance, I mostly
read about the war.

A newspaper ad encouraged Americans to conserve cooking
oil. THE JAPS STILL HAVE THE FATS the headline said. I wasn't sure
why fat was important to the war effort. But I was tired of the
word *Jap*. There was news of German atrocities in northern Italy
and articles on fighting in the Pacific. A place in the Vosges
Mountains of France called Bruyères was under attack by the
Allies. Aachen, a city in Germany, had been captured by our
troops. We were in Germany now? At least some of us? But
where was Mike?

More newspaper articles: three thousand Nisei enrolled in
colleges; Fifth Army using searchlights for night fighting in Italy;
Japanese fleet in trouble; crematorium for thousands of Nazi
foes, including many Jews, found in Holland; Nazis digging in,
laying new mines near Bologna, Italy; our casualties in Italy now
ninety thousand. But Mike wasn't one of them. Ninety thousand,
and somehow he had escaped. To what?

I thought of our camp population, swollen to twenty thousand now. I tried to imagine ninety thousand, all dead. Then I tried to forget.

Halloween came and went. November arrived, dark and windy and cold. Another letter came, dated October 25th. It was short, barely half a page of dirty paper, not even Mike's stationery, but I thanked everyone and everything for the words. He was still writing.

The weather remained bad, he said, the fighting worse. They'd pulled back to regroup, to rest, but sleep was hard to come by. "Now they've given us some kind of special assignment," he said, "but no one's saying what it is." The 2nd Battalion was getting ready to leave, Mike's 3rd and the 100th would be moving out in a day or two. "Everyone's on edge, trying to pass the time with rations and water and hollow laughter and snatches of sleep." He said he'd managed to get hold of a couple of Hershey bars and he was saving them for the mystery assignment. "I miss all of you," he said. "I can't wait to see you."

I kept at the newspapers. I read an article in the *Chronicle* about some seventeen-year-old American soldiers—twins— missing in action in Italy. Only three years older than me, and fighting. Missing. I remembered them to the stars that night. The November 6th *Chronicle* had an even more amazing story. A coast-guardsman was returning home to the United States after taking part in four South Pacific invasions. He'd lied about his age to join. He was fourteen. My age. I pictured myself lying about my age, getting assigned to the 442nd, moving up to the front line, crawl-ing into a foxhole next to Mike, taking up my position with my rifle at my shoulder, and having him look over and see me, just kneeling there as if I belonged. I pictured his smile, the way he'd get me in a headlock and tell me how glad he was to see me.

But would he be glad? Do well in school, he'd said. Go to college. Stay far away from uniforms and guns and war.

The same paper had an article about the rescue of a battalion of Texas soldiers that had been trapped behind enemy lines in the Vosges Mountains. The article didn't say who had rescued them, but I got a whisper of a feeling. I tried to work out in my head the timing, the location of what was happening over there. I wondered about Mike's secret assignment.

More news stories. With most of the votes counted, FDR—the man who had sent us away—was winning the 1944 presidential election. Allies were advancing in the Pacific, in Italy, Germany, France. American casualties in the battles in the Vosges Mountains were described as "light." I found comfort in that word.

Life had a photo of General MacArthur wading ashore in the Philippines. I studied the picture on the slim chance that Sandy could be in it. He wasn't. The same magazine had an article about German soldiers—prisoners of war—who had been captured in battle and imprisoned in Kentucky. Their prison—barbed wire, guard towers, tarpaper barracks, dirt, desolate countryside—looked just like Tule Lake.

A Saturday. Cold, dry, windy. I sat on the steps outside our barracks, waiting for the mail to be delivered to our block manager. I hoped for a letter from Mike, or Mae, or Sandy, or Ray. People walked by, bundled up against the weather. Guards drove past in their jeeps. Inside our room Mom and Dad and Grandmother sat, warming themselves by the fire, waiting for the next big event—supper—to take their minds off things for a while.

I looked up at the sound of a car approaching from the direction of the gate. It wasn't a jeep sound, and now that harvest was over, we didn't get much else in camp. After a few seconds I spotted a dusty, army-brown Chevrolet inching its way between the rows of barracks. It stopped next to one building, then moved on, sunlight glinting off its windshield.

My chest tightened. I had to work to get a breath. I'd seen this car before, or its twin. I prayed it would stop where it was, turn around, go back. And it did stop. But only temporarily. It was searching, on the prowl. Fifty yards away it jerked ahead again, and this time it angled toward our barracks, toward me. Its big grille was locked in an ugly grin.

It crept forward, closing ground, leaving a low wake of dust. Behind the windshield I could see the driver, the passenger. Soldiers, long-faced, heads held high.

I stood. I wanted to go inside and warn my family. I wanted to run. But maybe this wasn't what I feared. Maybe this was someone else's brother or son or grandson. Maybe it was Mike but he was just missing or captured or wounded. He'd gotten a flesh wound, like the good guys in the cowboy movies.

I fingered the smooth silver of the cross Mae had given me.

The car stopped ten feet away, close enough to spit at, to hit with a marble. I didn't do either. I just stared as the doors opened, as the two soldiers got out. The passenger carried a bulging manila envelope; the driver retrieved a package from the back seat. They closed the doors and moved together and stood, eyeing me. I waited for them to ask me directions to some other poor family's room.

"This the Hanada family's apartment, son?" the passenger said. He was an officer, one silver bar on his shirt collar. A lieutenant, and young. What did he know about stuff like this, anyway?

"Yes," I heard myself saying.

"Your folks in?"

"Why?" I said, but I knew they weren't going to tell me.

"We need to talk to your folks," the driver said. He took a couple of steps, walking with a limp. He had a young-old face and wore sergeant's stripes and a bunch of ribbons on his uniform coat.

"Just a minute," I said, and I opened the door and stepped inside and closed it behind me, leaving the two soldiers outside in the cold. My heart was pounding and I was sure I wouldn't be able to talk past the lump in my throat. Maybe if I didn't say anything, if I kept the door closed, they'd just go away.

Grandmother looked up from her flower making. I felt her eyes on me. She smiled that perfect white smile but then it disappeared. "What is it, Joseph?"

"Some soldiers," I said. My voice echoed around the bare room. Mom and Dad got to their feet at the sound of it. They moved toward me. "They're here," I said to them. "They want to talk to you."

Mom swallowed a sob. I heard it die in her throat. Grandmother rose and followed them, walking stiffly, as they moved toward the door. I opened it for them, waited for Grandmother to pass, and followed them out.

The soldiers were still there, in the same place, in the same positions, with the same sad faces, as if time had stopped once I'd gone inside. I looked past them, past their car. People walked by, hurrying once they took in the scene, looking away or down, out of respect, maybe, or fear that it could happen to them next, that it was catching.

"Mr. and Mrs. Hanada?" the lieutenant said. We stood in front of the soldiers on the hard ground, lined up like the targets of a firing squad, Dad on one end, then Mom, Grandmother, and finally, me. The lieutenant looked at Grandmother and nodded. "Ma'am."

"I am Michael's grandmother," she said, raising herself up to her full height. She knew why these soldiers were here.

The lieutenant nodded at her again. The sergeant looked at me. "This is his brother Joseph," she said. "He is too young to go in the army."

The lieutenant gave her a half-smile that turned sad. "I'm afraid we have bad news," he said. He glanced at a piece of paper—a letter—in his hand. "We've received notification that Private First Class Michael Hanada was killed in action in the Vosges Mountains of France while serving with the Third Battalion of the Four-forty-second Regimental Combat Team, United States Army." The words flooded out, but they hit like separate waves: crashing, crashing, crashing.

I heard soft noises from Dad and Mom but I didn't dare look at them. The lieutenant studied the paper. His fingers were trembling. Grandmother's arm went around my shoulders but I couldn't feel it. I felt numb. "He and the rest of his unit were engaged in an effort to free a battalion of soldiers which had become trapped behind enemy lines," he continued. "Private First Class Hanada and his fellow soldiers fought valiantly and against all odds. And they were successful."

He went on, talking about the importance of what they had

done to the overall war effort, the gratitude of the mothers and fathers of the soldiers who had been rescued, the medals that were likely to be awarded. His voice faded into the background as my mind drifted away. I thought about Mike's special mission. I recalled the article I had read about the lost battalion of Texas soldiers. I wondered who was responsible for their getting trapped, who had made the decision to send the battalions of Nisei in to get them out. Part of me wanted someone to blame. But what good would that do?

I dragged myself out of my thoughts and back to my nightmare. The soldiers were handing the letter and envelope and package to my parents, saying something about personal effects. Grandmother was crying to herself. I could feel her sobs. They spread to me. Through my tears I watched the soldiers turn and walk to their car. They got in and started off, making a slow half-circle before heading for the gate.

We came together—Dad, Mom, Grandmother, and me—in a knot of grief. Sounds of mourning poured out of our mouths and flowed around us like a deep moat. People continued to hurry past, going to supper or to visit friends or to read their latest letter from their own soldier. No one bridged the moat.

We skipped supper. We sat outside, immune to the puny chill in the air. It was dwarfed by the chill in our hearts.

Finally we moved inside to the warmth of the fire. Dad put Mike's things in a corner, unopened. We talked but said nothing. At first I expected an outburst from Grandmother, bitter words from Dad, a torrent of misery from Mom. Those things didn't happen, and when they didn't, I thought I understood why. This thing—Mike's death—was too big. What could match it?

We had had months to think about the possibility of Mike's dying, to prepare, but it had left us in shock anyway. What I saw on the faces of Mom and Dad and Grandmother, in their eyes, was numbness. And one other thing: watchfulness. They all seemed to be watching me, expecting me to crumble, waiting to put me back together. But I felt petrified, like a piece of ancient wood. I couldn't crumble.

I went to the wall and reread Mike's letters. Over and over. Starlight. The afterglow of a dead star.

No one read the newspaper; there was no need. We went to bed early and lay in the dark and listened to each other struggle for sleep. Grandmother slipped away first, then my parents, out of words to say to each other. I lay there longer, wide awake. Finally I found my flashlight and switched it on. I wrote. My feelings rose like a rain-swollen river. They spilled over, onto the pages of my journal.

EIGHTEEN

I woke the next morning to the sounds of my parents. They were sitting on the edge of Mom's bunk in the early light from the window, holding each other, sighing and sobbing and shaking their heads and murmuring to each other in Japanese. I looked around our shabby little room and tried not to tell myself that this was what Mike had died for. I closed my eyes and pretended to be asleep. Was Grandmother, lying so still next to me, doing the same?

I wondered if there was a way to make a trade, my life for Mike's. Maybe if I died and it would bring him back, my parents wouldn't be so heartbroken. And I wouldn't have to be, either. But even with my mind clouded with sleep and sorrow, I knew my parents loved me too. And I knew a trade wasn't possible.

Eventually I did fall back to sleep. When I woke, my parents were gone. To church, Grandmother said. I was glad they hadn't asked me. I wasn't happy with God. I had nothing to say to him. Not now. I no longer felt like a little kid, and maybe Mom and

Dad saw that. Maybe they were allowing me to make my own way, at least for a little while.

I got up, empty as a hobo's pocket, and went to breakfast with Grandmother. I felt people's eyes on me. Some of them came up and said they were sorry to learn about Mike. I watched their mouths move, but I heard the sounds of battle. I didn't know what to say back except thank you.

The day dragged on. I walked to the canteen with Mom, read a *Life* magazine, dug for shells. Anything to get my mind on something less painful than Mike's death. But I still kept picturing him over there, dying in some strange cold place, alone maybe. The soldiers hadn't said exactly how he died, so my imagination took over, choosing a lingering, cruel death one minute, a quick, merciful one the next. But none of them was merciful, really. I felt as if my heart were going to shatter like that long-ago marble.

I went to the fence that night with Dad. The stars came out, bright, mocking, daring me to make another wish.

So I did. I decided to go for broke. I wished for a safe and peaceful place for Mike; I wished I could see him again someday; I wished we would get to leave this prison soon; I wished for a new place for us to live where people judged us by what we did instead of how we looked.

Dad was quiet. "Mike helped save many lives," he said finally.

"Yeah," I said. I could see my breath in the cold air. "I wish someone would have saved his." But it was too late for that wish.

That night, after the lights were out and I thought everyone was asleep, I got out of bed and dressed and took my marbles out to the field where Mae and I had played so many times, where Mike and I had played before he left. In the moonlight I dug a hole with the shovel Sandy had given me. I buried the bag of marbles deep in the ancient soil and packed it down on top of them.

Dad was waiting for me in the shadows when I neared the barracks. I was glad to see him. I didn't feel as grown up just then. He put his arm around me, and without words, we went inside. We went to bed and listened to each other breathe.

The next morning I woke up early, before anyone. I tried to get back to sleep, to recapture a sweet, lifelike dream I had had in the night. But I couldn't sleep. I kept reliving the day before, the day before that. When first light came into the room, I wrote of those days.

I skipped school; my parents said nothing.

That afternoon, letters came in the mail—one for me from Mae, one for my parents from Mae's parents. Good news, finally. A wish granted, finally. "We have found a sponsor for you!" Mae wrote. "There is a job for your dad and a place for you to live." We would be leaving Tule as soon as final arrangements could be made with the government, moving to Ontario, Oregon, near Mae and her family. A few weeks, and we would be gone.

My heart felt lighter, up from the bottom of my chest. I would miss Ray, but I had gotten used to missing him. Mae would be my friend, and maybe there were other friends in Ontario I just hadn't made yet. I would miss the White River Valley, but I had a feeling it wouldn't miss me.

I saw sad smiles on my parents' faces, life in Grandmother's eyes. Mike's death would be with us forever, but maybe he had died for something after all. I wanted to believe that, even though I didn't feel it.

My parents wrote back to Mae's parents, thanking them for everything they had done. I wrote back to Mae. I told her about Mike, how I missed him. I told her I would keep my promise to teach her to whistle. But the rest of my letter was filled with thanks. I walked to the post office and mailed the letters.

When I returned to our room Grandmother was gone, doing laundry. Dad and Mom were also away, talking to reporters for the *Star* about an article on Mike, talking to Reverend Sakamoto about a memorial service.

I stoked up the fire in the stove and stood back, looking around the little room where we had spent more than two years of our lives, reminding myself we had only a few more weeks here.

Mike's belongings still sat in one corner, untouched. I stared at them for a minute, considering, wondering if anyone would care if I looked. Should I let my parents be the first to go through his stuff? But I decided that if they wanted to be first they would've looked by now, they would've warned me away. So I went to the corner and picked up the envelope and package and brought them to the table.

The envelope didn't contain much: the handkerchief with the river and trees Grandmother had made for Mike, the stone she had given him, my old school picture, some of the letters we had written to him, the Saint Christopher medal. Everything was dirty, water-streaked, wrinkled and bent and dog-eared. Except for the medal. It was shiny, as if someone had rubbed it clean, and I wondered why. Was it just mud that had been scrubbed away?

I put everything back and clasped the envelope shut. Pushing it aside, I turned my attention to the package. It was wrapped in brown paper, taped and twined. Government-issue packaging, I figured. I slipped off the twine and tore away two layers of paper. Inside was *The Red Badge of Courage*, dirty and battered. Under it was another book: Mike's journal.

I picked it up and thumbed through it, back to front. The pages were swollen and dirty and blank. Blank. Blank. All blank. Until I got to the beginning. At the top of the first page was a date: October 24th, 1944. Below the date was a poem. On the next few pages, over the next few days, he'd written other poems, some in pen, some in pencil, all of them streaked with grime. I nearly smiled at the thought of Mike avoiding his journal for so long, as if it were an extra helping of brined liver. I nearly cried at the thought of what monster-under-the-bed horrors finally drove him to start writing in it.

October 24th:
Death in the day, fear
At night. Hurry up and wait,
Hurry up and wait.

October 25th:
Freedom is a blind
Man, caning through a minefield.
Hear his tap-tap-tap?

October 26th:
Soldiers, fighting sleep,
Shiver under drenched blankets.
Frigid sun rises.

October 28th:
Blood spills, cherry-red,
From brown bodies. Do colors
Matter, in the end?

October 29th:
When freedom walks here,
Nisei can head home at last.
When will they be free?

When they die, I said to myself. When they die.

I read Mike's words again and again, until my throat was thick with sadness, until the lines blurred over. Then I sat with the journal open in front of me, waiting for my family to come back. Mom and Dad and Grandmother needed to read what Mike had written.

Dad returned first. The burden of talking about Mike weighed on his shoulders, making him look older. But when he saw me a smile crossed his face. I remembered his brave words when he'd just missed Mike's leaving: *I will enjoy Michael when he returns.*

I stood and gave him Mike's journal. "He wrote something," I said.

He handed me a small sack. The cloth was pure white and cinched at the top with orange string. "An exchange," he said. "You will need these now."

Weighing the distantly familiar contents of the sack, I waited for him to start reading Mike's words. Then I uncinched the string and looked. Marbles. New ones. Dozens of them. Surprise—and Dad's thoughtfulness—took my breath away.

These I would keep. These were free of the memories I found

more bitter than sweet. I watched Dad's face as I slipped my hand into the sack and let the smooth glass flow through my fingers. "Thank you," I said, grateful he didn't think me too grown up for this gift.

He nodded, eyes on the page. "Thank *you*, Joseph." He pulled a chair to the stove and sat with his coat still on, reading and rereading. I went to my bag and got out my journal. I sat in a chair next to him and added some words.

When he finally closed Mike's journal and set it carefully on the floor next to him, I handed him mine. "No one else has read it," I said.

"I am honored, then." His voice was watery, his eyes were spilling over. He moved his chair closer to mine and opened the journal. He read, the expressions on his face changing like the seasons, while my attention shifted back and forth between him and my marbles, while I removed each one from the sack and examined it in the firelight, imagining it as a pearl.

I wondered what he was thinking, what he would say when he was finished reading. I thought about Mae, about games of marbles in a different place, a free place, about leaving Tule Lake. I thought about Mike's dream for my future, the advice he had given me about school and college and writing.

I thought about my dream of the night before, the one I wanted never to forget, the one I had just written of in my journal.

In the dream Mike and I are back in our green valley, walking the banks of our lost river. I breathe in the cool spring air, smell the fresh smells of new life sprouting from trees and shrubs and ground. We toss a fir cone back and forth, laughing, until darkness sends us home.

Author's Note

Japan's 1941 bombing of Hawaii rattled the world like a monstrous earthquake, rolling gigantic shock waves across the Pacific. The waves couldn't be seen, but they were real and they had names. Disbelief. Sorrow. Fear. Anger. Hatred. They thundered against our shores and swept us into a deadly war with Japan and its European allies. And washed away the rights of thousands of our own people.

In the days just after the bombing, our government arrested many influential Japanese Americans living on the West Coast. Within a few months, their families and friends—entire populations of loyal residents and citizens—were being forced from their homes, processed through primitive assembly centers, and sent far away to live in backcountry internment camps. For most young men, the only way out of these camps, which at their peak held approximately 120,000 Japanese Americans, was by joining the army and fighting for the country that had turned its back on them.

Once given the opportunity, they volunteered by the thousands. They served in the Pacific, in North Africa, in Europe. Their bravery and accomplishments were unmatched. And they paid the price. The medal known as the Purple Heart is awarded to those who are killed or wounded in battle. Soldiers of the 442nd Regimental Combat Team, living—and dying—by their motto of Go for Broke, received over nine thousand Purple Hearts. They were awarded an equal number of other medals, including thirty-three Distinguished Service Crosses, the highest decoration for valor these soldiers were considered for in those days.

As a team, the 442nd received dozens of commendations, including seven Presidential Distinguished Unit Citations. At the end of World War II, when President Truman presented the last of these citations during a ceremony on the White House grounds, he spoke to the Nisei soldiers about the importance of what they had done. "You fought not only the enemy, but you fought prejudice, and you won."

Yet even after their accomplishments and sacrifices, Nisei soldiers and their families—those who had survived the war and endured the camps—came home to communities where many people still looked on them as the enemy, where resuming their lives meant starting over. Many of them had nothing to return to. Many of them decided not to return.

The Japanese American people of the White River Valley, near Seattle, were among those whose lives were forever changed.

It wasn't until 1976 that Executive Order 9066 was officially terminated. It wasn't until 1996 that Congress requested a review of the service records of dozens of Asian Americans and Pacific Islanders whose World War II heroics had been overlooked, ignored, or intentionally downplayed. As a result of that review, twenty Japanese American soldiers, many of whom were no longer living, were awarded the Medal of Honor, the highest award for valor given to members of the armed forces. The award ceremony took place in Washington, D.C., on June 21, 2000, fifty-five years after the war ended.